BAKER'S DOZEN

THE DO-GOODERS

BAKER'S DOZEN

THE DO-GOODERS

Created by Miriam Zakon
Written by Aidel Stein

Targum/Feldheim

First published 1994

Copyright © 1994 by Targum Press
ISBN 1-56871-049-6

Phototypeset at Targum Press

Printing plates by Frank, Jerusalem

Published by:
Targum Press Inc.
22700 W. Eleven Mile Rd.
Southfield, Mich. 48034

Distributed by:
Feldheim Publishers
200 Airport Executive Park
Spring Valley, N.Y. 10977

Distributed in Israel by:
Targum Press Ltd.
POB 43170
Jerusalem 91430

Printed in Israel

Contents

WHO'S WHO IN THE BAKER'S DOZEN

ASHER BAKER, *age 16. The eldest of the Baker clan, Ashi dorms in a nearby yeshivah — but still manages to take part in the family's adventures!*

BRACHA BAKER, *age 13. It's not easy being the oldest girl in such a large family, especially when you've got five famous sisters just two years younger than you are! But Bracha always rises to the challenge, usually with a smile. Her hobbies are reading, gardening (with her mother), and painting.*

RIVKA BAKER, *age 11. Eldest of the quintuplets, Rivka often tries to mother — and sometimes tries to boss around — her sisters. A talented guitar player with a beautiful voice.*

ZAHAVA BAKER, *age 11. With eleven brothers and sisters, Zahava still manages to get her way. A pretty girl, the kind who gets picked to play Queen Esther in Purim plays, she is usually good-natured, but sometimes high-strung. Her hobbies are drawing, fashion, and needlepoint.*

DINA BAKER, *age 11. Dini is as dependable as her sister Zahava is flighty. She hates injustice and defends the underdog in any fight. Her hobbies include reading and dancing.*

TIKVA BAKER, *age 11. Tikva is blind in one eye and has very poor eyesight in the other; still, she is fiercely independent. Though she cannot see at all in the dark, she refuses to walk with a cane. A very bright girl, she reads all her books in braille. She is shy and reserved with strangers, but at home everyone looks to her for advice and support. Tikva writes poetry in her spare time.*

YOCHEVED BAKER, *age 11. "The Baby Dynamo," as her father calls her, is the smallest of the quints, and a ball of energy and excitement. Yochie's always ready for adventure, quick to anger but quick to forgive. She loves schemes, the more outrageous the better, but rarely thinks about consequences until she's up to her neck in them. Her hobbies change with every new month.*

MOISHY BAKER, *age 9. "He's his father's genius, and my gray hairs," is the way Mrs. Baker describes her difficult prodigy. When he's in the mood, he can memorize hundreds of mishnayos; when he doesn't feel like it, he can fail every math test his teacher gives him. He collects coins and is a computer whiz.*

CHEZKY BAKER, *age 8. A jolly boy, always laughing, terrible in his studies but so good-natured about it that even his teachers have to smile. An expert softball player.*

DONNY BAKER, *age 5. A tough cookie, an independent kid who doesn't care what anyone else thinks of him.*

SARALEH BAKER, *age 3. A sweet little girl, with a dangerous tendency to wandering off.*

RACHEL AHUVA BAKER, *age 1. A fat baby, all cheeks and tummy and legs. She's usually smiling — and why not, with four fathers and seven mothers (besides Abba and Ima)?*

1
Hiding

Donny burst out of the cupboard under the kitchen sink and ran into the dining room. He slapped his hand down on the dining room table and shouted: "HOME FREE, HOME!" There was an anguished scream from the hall.

"Who was that?" Zahava plunged into the dining room. "Donny! How did you get in here? Where were you?"

Donny stuck his tongue out at his older sister, smiled and didn't say a word.

Zahava glared at him and started out of the room. Then she caught a glimpse of herself in a small mirror. She smoothed her straight black hair, straightened her collar and smiled at her reflection, showing her dimples. Even a good game of hide-and-seek wasn't a reason to look like a total wreck. Donny giggled at her. He thought Zahava was funny about clothes and stuff, but she was also a lot of fun to be with. She went out of the room to continue her search. Donny watched her go.

After she left, Donny sat on one of the dining room chairs and waited. She would find someone else soon, he was sure. The evening light shined through the open windows, tinting the room a gentle orange and highlighting the dark wood furniture. The air smelled fresh and warm.

Supper was over. Donny had eaten lots of mashed potatoes, his favorite, and his tummy felt comfortably full. Ima and Abba had gone out shopping and promised to bring back dessert. He swung his legs as he sat, kicking another chair and singing to himself.

"She didn't find me; she couldn't catch me," he chanted. "I'm only six, and she couldn't catch me. Ha, ha, ha!" He straightened his *kippah* on his fair hair and put his chubby cheeks in his hands, swinging his legs and kicking the chair harder and harder.

From upstairs he heard screaming and laughing and the pounding sound of running feet. Donny sat up. Who had Zahava found? Would they get away? The running feet came closer, and Yochie burst through the door.

"Home free, HOOOOOOME!" she sang out as she slapped the table. Donny bounced in his seat and shouted, "Yay!"

Zahava didn't bother to follow Yochie any further. They heard her feet running down the hall.

Yochie bounced up and down on her feet a few times, her short hair bouncing with her. A big smile spread across her face, and her dark eyes sparkled.

Donny eyed her appreciatively. Yochie was always a lot of fun, but, boy did she ever get into trouble!

Another quintuplet, Tikva, slipped into the room, her finger to her lips. She touched the dining room table and said: "Home free, home."

"You'll have to say it louder if you want Zahava to hear you," said Yochie.

Tikva grinned, and taking a deep breath she bellowed: "Home free, home!" They could hear Zahava shout "Oh no!" from somewhere in the direction of the homework room.

"Where did you hide?" Yochie asked Tikva.

"In the pantry," Tikva told her. "I put a case of wine on top of a case of soda, put a box of tuna next to it, and hid behind them. Zahava poked her head in but she didn't see me!" She giggled.

Donny swung his legs happily; he was glad that Zahava didn't find Tikva. He didn't think it was fair that Tikva was almost blind. Hide-and-seek isn't an easy game for an almost-blind person to play. That didn't stop Tikva from playing; she always thought of good hiding places. When she was "it" she would often find people with the help of her extra-good hearing. Tikva was very smart and very independent; Donny thought she was great.

They heard screams. Someone yelled, "I got you!" followed by a bumping noise.

"Sounds like someone fell down the stairs!"

They dashed out of the room and found Zahava and Rivka in a tangle on the landing between the first and second floors, laughing hysterically.

"Oh, oh, oh!" gasped Rivka. "Get off of my foot!"

"Help! Which is your foot?" Zahava cried. They all burst out laughing again. Donny laughed so hard he had to sit down.

"What happened?" Yochie demanded. While Zahava and Rivka disentangled themselves, Rivka explained, between gasps, "I hid in the linen closet. I didn't hear anyone, so I thought the coast was clear."

"Ho, ho, ho!" chortled Zahava, holding her sides.

"So I opened the door and there was Zahava! I screamed, and she screamed and jumped ten feet in the air." Rivka began to giggle again. "So I ran for the stairs and Zahava grabbed me at the top!" Rivka laughed so much she couldn't go on.

"Rivka was yelling and trying to pull away," Zahava continued for her. "Then I lost my balance and here we are!" Zahava laughed till tears came to her eyes.

Rivka rose slowly to her feet, straightening her long legs and smoothing her light brown hair. She pushed her glasses up her nose and grinned.

"Are you alright?" Tikva grinned, only mildly concerned.

"I think so," Rivka gasped. "I'm just not sure that I still have my own feet!" She went off into shrieks of laughter.

Donny liked to see her like this. Usually the eldest of the famous Baker quintuplets was so bossy and serious, always in charge, always making lists and stuff. This way was more fun. "Zahava didn't find me!" he told her.

"Good for you, Donny!" Rivka ruffled his hair.

"Home free, home!" They heard a call from downstairs.

"Oh no!" Zahava slapped her forehead with her hand.

They all charged into the kitchen.

There was Dini, waiting quietly, with three-year-old Saraleh on her lap. "What took you so long?"

"Zahava bumped into someone she knows and was held up," said Yochie with a grin.

"Ooooooh, Yochie!" Dini rolled her eyes at her sister. The two sisters looked alike, but their personalities couldn't be more different. Dini felt things deeply and would act on her strong feelings, protecting people and righting wrongs. It was just like her to hide with her younger sister and make sure she had fun.

"Should we call the others?" Rikva asked.

"Who's left?"

"Well, we have Rivka, Tikki, Dini, and Yochie and me. That's all of the quintuplets." Zahava counted off on her fingers. "And Donny and Saraleh. Ima and Abba and the baby are at the supermarket, and Ashi is in yeshiva."

"They weren't playing anyway," Donny pointed out.

"So that leaves Bracha, Moishy, and Chezky." Zahava ran to the door. "Ready or not, here I come!" She ran out of the room. Bracha stepped out from behind the dining room door. She walked over to the table, touched it, and called "Home free, home."

Everyone stared at her. "Bracha," said Rivka. "Bracha, you weren't behind that door the whole time, were you?"

"I'm not telling." Bracha crossed her arms and looked smug.

"You were. You were!" Donny grabbed her by the arm and jumped up and down. Bracha was his favorite babysitter of all of his sisters. Her face was round, and she had freckles across the nose, like him. Her hair was a little darker, and she wore it up in a ponytail that swung back and forth when she walked. She would read him stories, even when she didn't want to. Bracha was the oldest girl, and Donny was glad that she was often left in charge.

There was a noise next to the window. Everyone turned — just as Chezky climbed in. He jumped down from the window sill, narrowly missing one of Mrs. Baker's potted plants. He ran over to the table and shouted, "Home free, home!"

"Chezky, you weren't suppose to hide outside!" Dini frowned at her younger brother.

Good natured-Chezky looked surprised. "Really?"

"Don't you remember? We said that when we started," said Rivka with great patience.

"Oh." He flashed his big smile at them. "I guess I wasn't paying attention." Rivka bristled, then softened. No one could stay angry at Chezky for long. A miniature of their father, round and chubby, Chezky could win his way into anyone's heart.

"Now the only one left is Moishy," said Dini.

"I wonder where he is?" Rivka put her head around the corner and peeked out into the hall.

"Let's all go and look too — Zahava must need us to help by now." Yochie ran out of the room, pulling Tikva with her. Donny ran after them. They crawled all over the house looking for Moishy, who was nowhere to be found.

"Leave it to the mad genius to find the ultimate hiding place," moaned Zahava. Moishy, at nine years old, was the smartest in the family. Tall for his age, thin, with glasses and dark hair, he looked the part of the family *iluy*.

After a fruitless search, they congregated in the bedroom that Moishy shared with Ashi. Ashi, the biggest Baker kid, was away at yeshiva. His side of the room was neat as a pin. Moishy's side was not. There were projects on the floor, and the desk was full of papers. Laundry was piled on a chair, and the bed was not made.

Donny wandered over to the desk.

"Don't touch anything!" shrieked Yochie.

"I won't break anything." Donny was insulted.

"I wasn't worried about you breaking anything," Yochie explained. "It's just that something there might explode!"

"Or bite you," said Rivka with a sniff.

Donny backed away from the desk and looked around the room. They had looked everywhere, everywhere! Where could Moishy be? Out of the corner of his eye he saw the blanket on Moishy's bed move, just a little. Could it be...?

Chezky opened the closet door and hollered, "Moishy, we know you're in there! Come out with your hands up!"

"I give up!" said Zahava and plopped herself down on the bed. Suddenly, the blanket grabbed her. She screamed and struggled to get away. The other girls clutched at each other, laughing and shrieking. Donny jumped, startled, and then laughed. Chezky ran over to the bed and pulled off the blanket. There was Moishy with his face red and hair a mess from being underneath.

Zahava slid down to the floor and put her hands to her chest. "Oh, oh," she gasped. "I almost had a heart attack."

"*Chas v'shalom!*" said Dini. She turned to Moishy. "I can't believe that you were there! Here we were, looking everywhere, and you were there the whole time!"

"It's a good thing I didn't make my bed this morning." Moishy patted his blanket affectionately.

"This morning?" Rivka enquired archly.

"Are you trying to imply something, Miss Baker?" Moishy picked up his blanket and began to fold it in a fastidious manner.

"Who, me?" Rivka began.

Dini interrupted. "Come on. You're *it*, Rivka. Everyone down to the dining room!"

Down in the dining room, Rivka began to count. "One Mississippi, two Mississippi..." The family scattered.

"Not so fast!" Yochie shouted.

"Three-ee Mis-sis-sip-pi, fo-ur Mis-sis-sip-pi."
Rivka stretched out each word.

"Better!"

"Fi-ve Mis-sis-sip-pi — Chezky, only in the house!"
Rivka commanded.

"I know!" Chezky's voice came from somewhere
upstairs.

"Se-ven Mis-sis-sip-pi..." Rivka lowered her voice
and counted faster. "Eight Mississippi, nine Mississippi..."

Donny ran upstairs and opened the linen closet.
Chezky was inside! "Shhhh!" he hissed, and grabbed
Donny. Donny shook him off and ran down the hall.
Because Chezky hid outside last time, he didn't know
that Rivka already used this hiding place, Donny
thought. Rivka would look here for sure.

Maybe I should use Moishy's idea? he thought.
Nah, I made my bed this morning. Anyway, I don't
want to spend a long time under a stuffy blanket. He
turned to run downstairs and bumped into Dini.

"Oof, Donny!" She rubbed her stomach and consid-
ered her little brother. "Do you want to hide with me?"

"No thanks!" Donny flew down the stairs and into
the living room. The living room was a good place
because it was close to base, but there weren't many
places to hide. Should I try to squeeze under the
couch? Maybe I'll hide behind the curtains?...but
there's Saraleh sitting on the window seat with one of
her dolls! Donny stopped short.

"Aren't you playing hide-and-seek?"

"No," said Saraleh, stroking her doll. "Shmoooly was crying." Donny looked at the doll and then back at Saraleh; this would not be a good place to hide; Saraleh might tell where he was!

"Fifty-eight Mississippi, fifty-nine Mississippi." He could hear Rivka counting in the dining room. She was almost done!

Donny ran down the hall and into the blue guest room. There was the closet, empty and half-open; that was a good place! He ran into the closet and tugged the door. It wouldn't move. Then Donny remembered that the door was stuck and had been since they moved in.

"Ready or not, here I come!" Donny tugged frantically at the door and dragged it shut. A last pull and it clicked. "They'll never find me here," he thought with satisfaction. "Not in a million years."

The first place Rivka looked was behind the dining room door. No one was there. Next the kitchen: the pantry, under the table, under the sink. No one. Rivka rubbed her hands together.

"This is going to be good!" she said.

She crept back into the dining room and checked behind the door again. Someone could have snuck in, she thought. Mrs. Baker's studio, where she worked on her illustration jobs, was off-limits so Rivka went into the living room next.

"No one's in here," Saraleh informed her. "Donny was here, but he left."

Rivka went over to the curtain and casually looked behind it. "Why aren't you playing?" she asked her smallest sister.

Saraleh held up her doll. "Shmoooly was crying."

"Oh. Where did Donny go?" Rivka slid behind the couch to make sure no one was there.

Saraleh looked at her. "I thought I wasn't supposed to tell," she said.

Rivka sighed. "That's right, sweetie. See ya later."

"I'm not suppose to tell you where Yochie is either." Saraleh smoothed her doll's hair and held it close.

Rivka moved into the hall. If Saraleh knows where Yochie is, then she should be close by, she thought. Rivka tiptoed to the front closet and opened the door. She looked under the coats: no feet. Then something made her look up.

"Yochie!" There was Yochie, somehow wedged up on the shelf where they kept the hats. Rivka jumped up and tagged her. "How did you get up there?"

Yochie slithered down. "It wasn't easy. Too bad you thought of looking up."

They heard someone running down the hall. Rivka dashed away and saw Chezky disappearing into the dining room. "Home free, home!" he cried.

Rivka skidded to a halt; no use chasing someone who was already home. Suddenly Moishy appeared on the stairs. He saw Rivka, yelled, and fled. Rivka screamed and charged after him.

Moishy ran down the hall and into the homework room, Rivka hot on his heels. As he ducked through the door and around the big table he cried. "You'll never take me alive!"

"That's alright," Rivka growled at him through clenched teeth. "I'll take you any way I can get you."

They ran back and forth around the table, Moishy dodging Rivka's every attempt to capture him.

"Give it up, Moishy," Rivka said in an eerie voice. "You'll never get away!"

"That's what you think!" Moishy cried, and without warning he scrambled over the table and out the door. Rivka ran after him.

They pounded down the stairs and towards the dining room. The door was closed. Moishy ran to it and pulled.

"It's locked!" Rivka was coming closer. Moishy pounded on the door. "Who did this?!?"

Rivka came up to Moishy with a triumphant cry. At the last minute he ducked and ran into the kitchen, right into an armful of groceries held by his father. The groceries went flying, and so did Moishy. Rivka barely stopped herself in time.

"Moishy Baker! Just look at what you've done!" Mr. Baker's usually jolly features were stern and upset. Moishy looked around the kitchen and gulped. Cans were rolling everywhere, and a bag of flour had burst. A bottle of soda was spinning slowly and gently foaming out of the cap. Mr. Baker had some sort of pink powder all over his suit front.

"What a mess," Moishy whispered.

"What a mess? What a mess? That's the understatement of the year!" Mr. Baker dusted off his jacket with brusque movements. "What a mess....," he muttered.

By this time Rivka was joined at the door by Chezky, Yochie, and Saraleh. They looked at the scene in silent amazement. Then Yochie put her hand over her mouth, and Chezky's eyes began to twinkle. Rivka turned a snort into a cough. Mr. Baker looked up at them, eyes narrowed, but he didn't manage to keep a straight face. Soon they were all laughing.

He held out a hand to Moishy. "Get up, my boy. We have a little work to do." He pulled Moishy to his feet.

"I'll help." "Me too!" Soon everyone was helping to clean up.

Mrs. Baker walked into the kitchen through the back door, her slim figure dwarfed by the big bags of groceries she carried. "Ephraim," she began. "There are only two more bags in the car..." Then she noticed the mess. She looked at her husband and, hands on her hips, gave an exasperated sigh.

"It was the seven o'clock express," Mr. Baker explained. "Seems there was something wrong with the crossing signal."

"I see." Mrs. Baker shook her head and rolled her eyes.

"I'll get the bags from the car," Rivka volunteered.

"I'll help," said Yochie. They went out the back door.

Moishy gathered cans and stacked them neatly on the counter. Mr. Baker salvaged as much flour as he could and swept up the rest. The soda bottle rocked gently.

Mrs. Baker picked up the bottle and wiped the floor with a damp rag. "Where is everyone?" she asked Moishy.

"We were playing hide-and-seek, so I guess they're still hiding." He stacked the last can.

"Will you please go and find them?"

"Sure!" Just then they heard a cry of "Home free, home!" from the dining room. "There's Dini!" Moishy yelled. He went out to find the rest of his brothers and sisters.

Donny didn't come out when he heard his brother calling. "They're trying to fool me," he thought. "I'm not coming out; they have to find me!" He laughed quietly to himself.

Moishy led the rest of the family back into the kitchen. His mother was putting away the last of the groceries, with Yochie and Rivka's help. Mr. Baker was outside, locking up the car. "Saraleh won't come," Moishy told his mother.

"It's okay," she said, surveying her brood. "Where's Donny?"

"Probably still hiding," Moishy joked.

Mrs. Baker smiled. "Really, where is he?"

"Probably playing with Saraleh," said Rivka.

"That's alright," said Mrs. Baker. "Don't bother him. What I have to say doesn't really concern him anyway."

Mr. Baker came into the kitchen. "It's such a beautiful night," he said to his wife. "Let's go sit out on the grass, and you can tell the kids what you wanted to tell them."

"What do you want to tell us?" Yochie asked.

"Where is the snack you got?" asked Chezky.

"The snack is the box of bakery cookies in the fridge, and I'll tell you what I want to tell you when we're all settled outside." Mrs. Baker pointed to the back door.

"Let's have lemonade," said Rivka. She went to a cupboard and took down a pitcher.

"If you were going to make it out of that pink powder, forget it," said Mr. Baker. "Unless you want to drink my suit."

"No, thank you!" said Rivka. "Besides, this is real lemonade. Tikva made it this afternoon."

"Real lemonade from real lemons?" Mr. Baker asked.

"Yup!"

"Imagine that!" Mr. Baker licked his lips.

"Yum!" said Moishy. "I'll bring the cups."

Soon the Bakers were settled on the grass. Mrs. Baker sat quietly on a big, low garden chair, her children sprawled around her. Mr. Baker stood with his cup in his hand, admiring the group.

"What's up, Ima?" Yochie asked.

Upstairs in the closet, Donny was singing to himself. "They can't find me, and they can't find me! They can't find me, and they can't find me!" He put his ear to the door and listened. It was very quiet.

"They must be looking in the basement," he said with satisfaction, and went back to his singing.

After awhile he put his ear to the door again. It's very quiet, he thought. I wonder if they're still looking. Maybe I'll peek a little.

Donny put his shoulder against the closet door and pushed gently, intending to open it very quietly. The door didn't move. He shoved harder. It still didn't move. He turned the knob and pushed. The door wouldn't budge.

Donny took a deep breath and pushed with all his might. The door stayed there as if it was a wall. He backed up a little and rammed himself into the door. The door didn't budge.

Donny began to get scared. He kicked the door and kicked it again. He jiggled the handle up and down and then swung on it, putting all his weight into his swing. I'm stuck, he thought in a panic. I'm locked in. I can't get out!

"Riiivka! Zahaaaava! Come and get me!" he called. "RIVVVVVVVKAAAA! COME AND GET ME!!!!!" Where are they? He looked around in the dark and felt his throat constrict with fear.

"Help! Help! HEEEEEELP! I'm stuck in the closet!" Donny banged and kicked the door. He kicked as hard as he could; for sure they would hear that!

He stopped for a minute and listened, putting his ear to the door and holding his breath. He didn't hear a thing. A small whimper escaped his lips. Then, frantically, he banged and called, banged and called. Where was everyone, and why weren't they coming?

2
. . . and Seeking

Mrs. Baker looked at the children sprawled around her. Yochie was trying to whistle on a blade of grass. Dini and Tikva were engaged in earnest conversation. Zahava was twirling a lock of hair around and around her finger, a smile playing on her lips. Rivka was laughing at Moishy and Chezky, who were thumb wrestling. Only Bracha looked unhappy, and Bracha was the one most on Mrs. Baker's mind.

I'm used to my Bracha being one of the more cheerful ones, she thought. I hope my idea will get to the bottom of whatever's bothering her; she's been out of it for more than a week.

She and her husband had discussed it in the car, and they both felt that Bracha's mood was the final pull to put this plan into action. Mrs. Baker cleared her throat to speak, and every head turned, except Bracha's. She seemed miles away.

"What I want to tell you is the following: I think I haven't been spending enough time with you. That is, each of you individually. You know, 'Ima time,' " Mrs. Baker's eyes moved around the group of children and rested on Bracha. Bracha, only half-paying attention, didn't notice. "So I've decided what we need is days 'off.' Really, days 'on.' I'll be taking each one of you out alone, without any of the others, to spend some time together." She sat back and waited for a reaction.

"Now that's what I call an idea!" said Zahava.

"Ditto!" said Rivka.

"Triple ditto!" Yochie crowed.

"What happened to double ditto?" quipped Mr. Baker.

"Boys too, or only quints?" asked Moishy.

"Of course, boys too!" Mrs. Baker was surprised by Moishy's question. "Everyone but Donny and Saraleh. They're home all afternoon and get plenty of time with me."

"Can we go anywhere?" asked Dina.

"I know where I want to go...," Zahava chattered excitedly.

The idea was a good one, thought Mrs. Baker. They're really excited. She looked at her husband, winked, and let the children talk. Bracha was the reason for this, she thought. How is she reacting?

She frowned a little as she looked at her eldest daughter. Bracha was sitting quietly, looking preoccupied, as she had for the past week or so. Not only preoccupied, thought Mrs. Baker, but also sad.

"Bracha?" Mrs. Baker called her gently.

Bracha looked up and tried to smile.

Mrs. Baker smiled her warm smile back and said, "We'll start with you first, honey, if you'd like."

Bracha looked uncomfortable. The chatter around them slowed down and stopped.

"It's okay, Ima, I don't have to be first..." Bracha moved uneasily. "I'm...I'm kind of busy this week and, well, let someone else go," she added.

Zahava jumped at the opportunity. "I have nothing to do this week, nothing at all! I'll be first!" She bounced as she spoke.

"Okay, honey," Mrs. Baker said to her, but she was looking at Bracha, her forehead wrinkled. Mr. Baker looked at her too, a small frown on his face. Everyone began to feel uncomfortable.

"It's getting chilly," Dina commented.

"I think I forgot something in the car," said Mr. Baker.

"I'll go with you," Moishy jumped to his feet.

Rivka began to gather up the cups; Bracha took the empty pitcher. The children filed into the house, chattering happily. Mrs. Baker followed them slowly.

Moishy and Chezky skipped past her, Moishy carrying a forgotten bag of groceries. Mr. Baker came up behind them.

"How do you think the meeting went?" Mr. Baker asked his wife quietly.

"Not exactly as I expected." Mrs. Baker stopped walking. "Bracha was amazingly unenthusiastic."

"I wonder what's bothering her." Mr. Baker shook his head. "I would have thought she would jump at the idea."

Mrs. Baker shook her head too. "I don't know." She looked around her. "By the way, have you seen Donny?"

After one more frantic flurry of action, kicking, pounding, and yelling, Donny gave up. He slid down with his back to the door and pushed his knuckles into his eyes, trying not to cry. His throat hurt from shouting, and his hands hurt from pounding. His feet hurt too. And his stomach. I hate it in here, he thought. I hate it! I want to get out!

After awhile, he opened his eyes and sniffed, wiping his nose on his sleeve. Peering ahead, he tried to see, but it was completely dark. There was no keyhole, and only the slightest glimmer of light where the door met the frame. Donny remembered his father saying how well the house was built and how strong it was. He kicked his foot angrily. Stupid house!

Straining his ears, he tried to listen. He thought he heard a shuffling noise. "Yochie? Bracha?" he called "Anybody?"

He heard the noise again. It wasn't from outside. It was in the closet, with him. What was it? A mouse? A rat? Donny moved and listened again. Oh, it was my foot! He settled back against the door.

Here in the dark I can't see, he thought. Anything could be here in this closet with me. There could be spiders, big black spiders, and I can't see them. He pushed his back hard against the door and rolled himself into a ball.

A cat can see in the dark, he thought as he looked. I wish I was a cat. Can a lion see in the dark? A tiger? I'll bet a monster can see in the dark. A monster. I hope there aren't any monsters in here. Donny put his head down on his knees and squeezed his eyes shut.

Ima says there's no such thing as monsters. Abba too. There can't be a monster in here. Donny felt a lump come up in his throat. Tears rolled down his cheeks and, quietly he began to cry.

I want Ima... I want Abba... I want to get out of here. I'm alone, and it's dark.

Donny cried for what seemed like a long time. He began to feel tired. His hands relaxed, his legs began to unwind, then he caught himself and rolled up in a ball again. This happened a few times. Then, without even realizing, he lay down, his back still against the door.

As he fell asleep, a thought came to him. *Hashem could get me out of here. I could daven to Hashem... My rebbe says a* tefillah *for someone who is sick. He says it's for people in trouble. "Ya'ancha Hashem b'yom...b'yom... Hashem, get me out of here, please... Ya'ancha Hashem..."* His lips stopped moving, and he fell asleep.

"That is really all of the groceries!" Mrs. Baker put the last box on a shelf, went out of the pantry, and closed the door.

"Yay!" Yochie ceremoniously crumpled a paper bag and threw it in the garbage.

"Yochie, why didn't you save that bag?" Dina asked her.

"It had a hole in it," Yochie replied. "I think."

"Don't worry about it," said Mrs. Baker. "We have plenty of paper bags." She looked up at the kitchen clock. "Wow, it's late! I've got to get Saraleh and Donny into bed. Who's seen them?"

"Saraleh is in the living room," Yochie said, pointing.

Mrs. Baker walked into the living room and found Saraleh on the window seat, with her doll.

"Bedtime, *ziskeit*," said Mrs. Baker softly.

"Shmoooly is already sleeping," Saraleh told her.

"Do you want to take him up to his bed?"

"No, it will wake him up," Saraleh thought for a moment. "I want to sleep down here."

Mrs. Baker pretended to think about this. "No, Saraleh, I don't think so. You belong in your bed."

"I could bring my blanket," Saraleh tried to persuade her mother. "I could bring Shmoooly's blanket."

"No, Saraleh."

Saraleh gave up with a little sigh and held her hands out to her mother. Mrs. Baker helped her jump off the window seat and led her upstairs.

"Have you seen Donny?" she asked on the way.

"I saw him, but he didn't want to hide in the living room," Saraleh told her.

"That was a long time ago." Instead of going to Saraleh's room, Mrs. Baker went down the hall to the homework room where Bracha and the quintuplets, except Yochie, were doing their homework. "Has anyone here seen Donny?"

"Not since hide-and-seek," Dini said.

"He didn't sit outside with us," Tikva remembered.

"Do you think he's still hiding?" Zahava asked.

"Impossible! The game was over an hour ago," said Bracha. "Donny! Donny!" she yelled.

"I'll go look in his room." Mrs. Baker went down the hall to the room Donny shared with Chezky. The door was closed so she knocked.

"Just a minute!" called a voice, and the door opened. "Oh, it's Ima! Come in!"

"Is Donny in here?" Mrs. Baker was beginning to feel impatient.

"Nope," said Chezky. "Haven't seen him."

Mrs. Baker hurried down the hall to Moishy's room. The door was open.

"Moishy, have you seen Donny?"

Moishy looked up from a project, surprised by his mother's tone of voice. "No, I haven't seen him, Ima."

"Well, where *is* he?" Mrs. Baker curled up the side of her mouth and looked to one side.

"Do you want me to help you look?" Moishy volunteered.

"Yes, please."

Moishy got up and went out of the room. Mrs. Baker took Saraleh to her own room and began to get her into pajamas.

When the other children heard that Donny still hadn't been found, they joined in the hunt. Mrs. Baker finished getting Saraleh ready for bed and went out into the hall, where she snagged Chezky.

"Any luck?" she asked.

"We're still looking," said Chezky and bounced off.

"Donny, come OUT; the game is OVER!" Yochie called.

"He can't still be hiding," Mrs. Baker protested.

"Maybe he's stuck somewhere," said Rivka, a hint of panic in her voice. The Bakers redoubled their efforts.

Moishy stopped Chezky. "We've got to do this systematically," he said. "We'll start at the bottom of the house. We'll look in each of the rooms, in order. First we'll call, listen well, and call again. Then we'll look under the beds, in each closet, and behind curtains."

"Sounds good to me." Chezky and Moishy ran down the stairs to the basement.

"This place is such a mess. Do you think he hid here?" Chezky toed an old piece of cardboard with his sneaker.

"We have to try everywhere." Moishy peeked into boxes and behind old chests. When they had looked everywhere, they called, "Donny!" and stood quietly to the count of ten, listening. When they were sure they didn't hear an answer they called again.

"Next, the blue guest room!" They clambered up the stairs. All over the house they could hear people calling.

Donny woke with a start. Where was he? In the horrible closet! Wait! Did he hear voices? Was someone calling his name?

"I'm here; I'm here!" Donny yelled, and banged on the door. "I'm here!"

Chezky and Moishy came into the room. "You look under the bed," Moishy was saying. "We don't have to look in the closet because..." Then they heard the noise.

"I'm here; I'm here!" They saw the handle of the closet shake.

"Donny!" "In the closet!" they said simultaneously. They ran over to the door and tried to open it.

"Get me out! Get me out!" They could hear him crying as he banged on the door with his hands and feet.

"We're coming, Donny!" Chezky shouted. "Who knows how long he's been in here?" he wondered with wide eyes as they struggled with the door.

"Get me out!"

"We can't open it," panted Moishy, giving up. "I'll run and get Abba — you keep trying." He ran out of the room.

Chezky put his head to the door. "Donny!" he bellowed. "Donny, listen!" Donny stopped banging. "Moishy went to get Abba; he'll get you out! Abba is coming!"

He could hear Donny sniff through the door. "Abba?" he said in a quavering voice.

"Yes!" Poor kid! Chezky thought. They'd better hurry!

Mr. Baker burst into the room, followed by the rest of the family.

"Here's Abba!" Chezky cried.

"Abba!" Donny called through the door. "Get me out of here!"

"Okay, Donny," said Mr. Baker in a reassuring voice. "We're going to get you out." He tried the door, giving it a good tug. "This is stuck."

"No joke," muttered Moishy.

"How did he get this door closed?"

"With Donny, where there's a will there's a way," said Mrs. Baker grimly. "Now, can we get the door open?"

"Moishy, get my tools." Moishy ran out and was soon back, lugging a big tool box. Mr. Baker selected a large screwdriver and began to pry open the door. There was a cracking noise, and part of the door came away.

"You'll break the door!" said Zahava.

"Who cares!" Dini clasped her hands and twisted them together.

Donny banged on the door again.

"Don't do that, Donny," said Mr. Baker. "Let me take care of it."

There was another crack.

"It's opening!" Yochie jumped up and down in her excitement.

"Get away from the door, Donny," Mrs. Baker called.

"It's going to open towards us, " Mr. Baker grunted. "You never know."

From all around the door there came a crunching sound as the door wrenched open a crack. Mr. Baker grabbed onto the edge and pulled; Chezky and Yochie jumped in to help him. Donny pushed from the inside. The door creaked open until there was just enough room for Donny to squeeze out.

"Oh, you poor baby!" wailed Rivka when she saw him.

"I'm not a baby!" Donny's hair was rumpled, his eyes red and his cheeks smeared with dust and tears, but he looked up at his big sister defiantly.

"You must have been so scared!" said Dini.

"No," said Donny shortly.

"You weren't scared?" Rivka looked at him doubtfully.

"No."

Mr. Baker reached down and squeezed his shoulder. "That's my boy!"

"I wasn't scared," said Donny again as Mrs. Baker picked him up. He let her hold him close. "I wasn't scared."

"Hmm," said Mr. Baker.

"It's past Donny's bedtime," said Mrs. Baker. "Come, Donny, have a hot chocolate before you go to sleep."

"No thanks," muttered Donny in a low voice.

Mrs. Baker helped Donny into bed. After Shema, he didn't seem to want her to stay.

"Okay, *ziskeit*," Mrs. Baker kissed him. When she got to the door of the room, Donny said: "Don't turn out the light."

"What?" Mrs. Baker turned.

"Don't turn out the light," Donny repeated. "Please," he added politely.

"Don't turn out the light?" Mrs. Baker scrutinized her son, small and round under the covers. "Alright, Donny, I won't turn it off."

"I wasn't scared," said Donny.

"Okay." Mrs. Baker kissed him and smoothed his hair. With a small sigh she went out of the room.

Chezky came to bed a little while later. Donny was lying with his face to the wall, breathing softly. Chezky tried to be very quiet in order not to disturb him. He got into his pajamas and draped his clothes on a chair, tiptoed out to wash up and tiptoed in again. After he said Shema he went to turn off the light.

"Don't turn off the light."

Chezky looked over to Donny's bed. Donny was still facing the wall; had he been awake the whole time?

"But, Donny, it's time to go to sleep." Chezky walked over to Donny's bed. "We have to turn off the light."

"Don't turn off the light."

Chezky sighed. "Alright, Donny, just this once." He got into bed and, wrapping his pillow around his head, he tried to go to sleep.

In the middle of the night, Chezky sat bolt upright in bed, his heart pounding. The light was off, and the only illumination came from the night-light in the hall. Chezky didn't know what woke him until he heard Donny scream again.

Chezky jumped out of bed and ran over to his younger brother, who was kicking his legs and thrashing around.

"Donny," he said in a loud whisper. "Donny, wake up!" He took Donny by the shoulder and shook him. He was rewarded with a clout in the head. Donny screamed again.

Mrs. Baker ran into the room, followed by Mr. Baker doing up his robe. She took Donny in her arms and held him.

"Shhh, shhh," she said as she stroked his head. "It's okay; here's Ima." Donny quieted down in her arms.

"Wh-who turned off the light?" he whimpered.

"I'm sorry, honey. Abba and I did. You were sleeping so peacefully when we made the rounds, we were sure you wouldn't mind."

The little boy rubbed his damp cheek. "It was so dark..."

"Shhh. It's alright now," soothed Mrs. Baker.

Donny was still sniffing and sobbing when the rest of the family, one by one, began to show up.

"What happened?" asked Rivka in a sleepy, frightened voice.

"Shhh," whispered Mrs. Baker.

Mr. Baker herded them out of the room. "Donny had a bad dream."

"Some bad dream!" said Rivka.

"I thought something horrible had happened," Bracha yawned.

"Poor baby," said Zahava.

"He's not a baby," Dini retorted.

"You know what I meant."

"Shhh!" said Mrs. Baker from the bedroom.

"Back to bed," said their father in a loud whisper. "Back to bed."

"Do you think he had the nightmare because he was locked in the closet?" Tikva asked.

"Who knows? Maybe," said Mr. Baker. *"Back to bed!"*

"Shhh!" said Mrs. Baker from the bedroom.

Mr. Baker hunched up his shoulders and tiptoed down the hall.

Chezky watched his mother put Donny back in bed and cover him. He could feel his heart still pounding. That was some scream, he thought. That must have been some nightmare.

Mrs. Baker, once she felt sure Donny was asleep, went to the door.

"Don't turn off the light."

Mrs. Baker sighed. "Chezky, do you mind if we keep the light on?" she whispered. "I'm sure it's just for tonight."

"Okay. I hope so." Chezky buried his head in his pillow again. "Goodnight," he said in a muffled voice.

"Goodnight, Chezky. Thank you."

3
Chezky's Diary #1

CLICK *CLICK* Testing one, two, three. Testing one, two, three. *CLICK* *CLICK*

I'm whispering because it's two o'clock in the morning, and I don't want anyone to wake up again. Again, you ask? Listen, diary, and I'll tell you all about it.

Ima and Abba went to the supermarket after supper, and while they were gone, we played hide-and-seek. It was a great game, anyway, until about an hour after it finished. That was when we found out that Donny was missing!

Well, we looked and we looked, and I thought Ima was ready to call the police when Moishy and I found him, believe it or not, in that closet in the blue guest room. That closet door was warped and never really closed right. Guess what little Donny did? That's right, somehow he managed to close it with himself inside! The door got stuck, poor kid, and he couldn't get out. He must have been in there for over an hour.

When we found him we couldn't get the door open, so we ran for Abba. He pried it open with a screwdriver: the door practically fell to pieces before it opened. Out comes Donny, a mess. But, boy, is he tough. He kept saying that he wasn't scared.

Ima put him to bed. He wouldn't go to sleep with the light off. When I came to bed he wouldn't let me turn it off either. I guess someone turned it off later, because when he woke up from a huge nightmare it was dark. Boy, did he scream! Even I was scared.

Well, after awhile he went back to sleep (along with the rest of the family, who all came running when they heard the scream). He went back to sleep with the light on, of course. I wrapped my pillow around my head and figured I could put up with this for a night or two.

I'm just about asleep when someone crawls into my bed. Who is it? That's right, Donny. He didn't say a word, just crawled in and went to sleep. I thought of kicking him out, but I figured if he was that scared maybe I should leave him alone.

Did you ever try to sleep with a six-year-old? He takes up more than half the bed (don't ask me how), and he moves. Arms and legs everywhere! I couldn't sleep...

So here I am in the study. I guess I should go back upstairs and get into Donny's bed...though he'll probably crawl in there with me.

CLICK

4
Oodles of Chesed

"So, kids, what's new?" Mr. Baker took a forkful of meat loaf and looked around the table expectantly.

"We have a great new project at school," Yochie began.

Moishy rolled his eyes to the ceiling and groaned. Yochie turned on him. "What's wrong with you?" she asked.

"Every time you have one of your projects, the whole family is turned upside down." Moishy stabbed several peas with his fork. "I don't see why you can't just learn. Isn't that why we send you to school?"

"Moishy!" Dini put down her fork and looked at him reprovingly.

"Just learn, huh?" Rivka snarled. "Just learn? Haven't you ever heard of 'derech eretz kadmah la-Torah'?"

"Really, Moishy." Rivka frowned at him and crossed her arms. "Do you think that memorizing *mishnayos* is the only *avodas Hashem*? There's *bein adam laMakom* and *bein adam l'chaveiro*, you know!'

Moishy looked bewildered. "What does this have to do with what I said?"

"Because this project is a *chesed* project!" said Tikva triumphantly.

"It's really a great idea." Yochie spoke quickly, one word tumbling over the other. "Each girl is going to pick a *chesed* to do and spend at least two hours a week on it! You can do almost anything, like babysitting, shopping for someone, volunteering..." Yochie counted off on her fingers.

"How about housework?" said Mr. Baker as he sprinkled salt on his potato.

"Oh, Abba!" Yochie wiggled with exasperation. Turning to her mother she said, "We're supposed to work on it till just before Lag Ba'Omer. Then each girl will report to the class about what she did." She grabbed her mother's arm.

"This is such a good idea!" Mrs. Baker tried in vain to steady her fork as she smiled at Yochie. Peas rolled in all directions. "It really helps to do *chesed* when everyone is doing it together..."

"And our teacher has so many good ideas!" bubbled Rivka. "When she first started talking about it, I thought some of the ideas were a little — oh, I don't know, strange — but then she told us how much you can learn from each act of *chesed* and how much you can give."

"Like if you babysit," said Zahava. "Not only are you helping, but you're also learning about children and patience and stuff like that."

"Or if you volunteer somewhere," said Tikva. "Then you learn all about the place and people you're volunteering for."

Mr. Baker nodded in agreement. Mrs. Baker beamed at her girls.

"Our teacher said that one of the most important things when you do *chesed* is to give the person exactly what he needs, For example," Dini explained, "if someone needs you to fold the laundry, then doing the dishes isn't helping."

"That's important," said Mrs. Baker.

"Or if they need some shopping done," she continued, "then weeding the garden isn't really *chesed*."

"Why not?" asked Moishy. He had finished eating and was following the conversation closely. "I mean, if the garden needed weeding, then you still helped."

Dini hesitated. "Look, if I need something done, and I need it done so badly that I even need help, and it really doesn't make a difference if other jobs aren't done, then how much of a *chesed* could doing the other job be?"

Moishy blinked. "What?"

Dini thought again. "If I need someone to watch my children because I have the flu, and I don't care if the garden gets weeded in a week or a month, but I really do need a nap, then weeding isn't much of a *chesed*, is it?"

"Very good, Dini!" Mr. Baker nodded at her approvingly.

"That's using your head," said Mrs. Baker. "Does anyone want some more potatoes?" Several children said yes. Mrs. Baker served the children closest to her and passed the platter.

"I don't see what they're getting so worked up about," muttered Moishy to Chezky.

"Huh?" said Chezky. He put a half a potato in his mouth.

"You'd think they owned all the *chesed* in the world."

"Mmmm," agreed Chezky, now that he'd figured out what Moishy was talking about. He would have said more, but his mouth was full.

"We'll be doing so much *chesed*," said Yochie. "We'll really be doing our part in '*olam chesed yibaneh*.' "

"Terrific!" Mr. Baker exclaimed.

Moishy had had enough. "You don't have a monopoly on *chesed*, you know." He crossed his arms and sat back.

"Yeah!" echoed Chezky.

The girls looked at them, open-mouthed.

"You're not the only ones who can do it," Moishy went on.

"Yeah!" echoed Chezky.

The girls still looked at him. Yochie began to get steamed up.

"We could do as much as you," Moishy went on. "And we don't need someone to assign us to do it."

"Yeah!" Chezky grinned a challenging grin at his sisters.

"Yeah!" Everyone turned in surprise to stare at Donny, who had decided to take sides with the other boys.

Yochie rolled her shoulders and cleared her throat. "I don't know how much time you'll be having," she said airily.

"What do you mean?" asked Moishy suspiciously.

"Well..." Yochie looked down at the table and toyed with her fork, a smile playing at her lips. "The world doesn't stop turning around."

"What?"

"There will still be chores to take care of around the house. We'll be terribly busy..." The other quints eyes' gleamed as they followed Yochie's logic.

"Oh no," Moishy flared. "Oh no, we won't be able to take care of your stuff! *We'll* be busy!"

"Yeah!" said Chezky.

"Yeah!" said Donny.

"Busy? Busy doing what?" Yochie demanded.

"Yeah, what?" asked Chezky, confused.

Moishy kicked him under the table. "What indeed, you may ask? Why, more *chesed*, of course!" Moishy leaned forward and banged his fist on the table.

"Yeah!" said Chezky.

"Yeah," Donny echoed.

"Wonderful!" said Mr. Baker. He had been following the conversation and was looking for an opportunity to diffuse some of the tension. "We could make it a family-wide project!"

"What a great idea." Mrs. Baker smiled at her husband.

"But it's our school project!" Yochie couldn't believe her ears.

"We can't have everyone doing *chesed!*" Zahava spread her arms wide to encompass the entire family, accidently hitting Bracha in the face and sending her glasses flying. "Oh sorry, Bracha!" She jumped under the table to retrieve her sister's glasses. Bracha rubbed her nose.

"Why not?" asked Mr. Baker.

"Because," came Zahava's voice from under the table. "Because..." She surfaced, Bracha's glasses in her hand. "Because..."

"Who will take care of the house?" Rivka finished for her. Zahava gave Bracha her glasses and looked at Rivka gratefully.

"Did you really think that you would stop taking care of the things you're responsible for because you were involved with this project?" Mrs. Baker raised her eyebrows in surprise.

Yochie opened and closed her mouth like a fish. Rivka wrinkled her forehead. The other quints looked serious.

"I want everyone to understand this," said Mrs. Baker, looking sternly around the table. "Being involved in this project, like any other project, in no way excuses anyone from his or her chores. Do I make myself clear?"

"Yes, Ima," whispered Dini. The other children nodded.

"But it's still our project," protested Yochie. "The boys don't have to interfere."

"We won't get in your way," said Moishy. "We'll be busy doing *chesed*."

"Yeah!" said Chezky.

"Yeah!" said Donny.

"Hush," said Mr. Baker. "I don't think they will bother you. Why don't you try and be happy that you were the reason someone else wanted to do extra mitzvos?"

Yochie was taken aback. Moishy looked smug.

Mr. Baker lifted his glass of water. "Here's to the Baker *chesed* project. May it spread happiness and light to us and all of Bloomfield!"

"Amen." Mrs. Baker raised her glass too.

One by one the children raised their glasses, but, as the boys eyed the girls and the girls eyed the boys, the responses to the toast were less than enthusiastic.

"Now," said Rivka as she looked down her list. "Here are all of my possibilities." She pointed to each one with her pencil as she went down the list again.

A. Babysitting
   1. The Kleins
   2. The Feldbaums
   3. The Feivelsons.

"You can skip the Feivelsons," Tikva told her. "I happen to know that Baila Wolf is already babysitting for them." Tikva was sitting on her bed, going through some of her old Braille books. She was hoping to volunteer at the local Center for the Blind and thought that the books might come in handy.

Rivka sighed and crossed off the Feivelsons and continued to the next list.

B. Volunteering
   1. The library
   2. The *gemach*
   3. Tutoring

"What would you do at which *gemach*?" Tikva asked her.

"The clothing *gemach*, the one that sends clothes to Eretz Yisrael," Rivka told her. "Sorting and folding, a little mending."

"Sounds good." Tikva nodded her approval. "Anything else on the list?"

"That's all for now." Rivka flipped the page on her pad. "Here's the list of phone numbers I have to call."

"Please don't read that to me!" Tikva said in mock horror.

Rikva laughed. "Fear not!" She got up and went to the study.

Opening the study door she found Yochie talking on the telephone. Dini and Chezky were sitting around looking bored.

"Okay, Mrs. Feldbaum. I'll call back in about an hour," Yochie was saying. "Goodbye." She hung up.

"What were you talking to Mrs. Feldbaum about?" Rivka asked her.

"About babysitting," Yochie answered. "She's got all these kids, and her husband travels a lot."

"I know," Rivka sighed, and, taking out her list, crossed off the Feldbaums.

"Are you finished with the phone?"

"Nope." Yochie picked up the receiver and dialed.

"Anyway, there's a line," Dini told her.

"You're waiting?" Rivka looked at her in dismay.

"Me too," said Chezky.

Rivka looked at them for a minute and decided to go down to the kitchen to get a snack.

Moishy was in the kitchen, sitting next to the telephone with the receiver next to his ear and his finger on the disconnect button. Every once in a while he would pick up his finger to see if the telephone was still in use. He ate pretzels as he waited.

Rivka helped herself to a cup of juice and sat drinking and watching Moishy. "What project are you hoping to do?" she asked him.

"I want to speak to the *gabbai*. Maybe there is something I could do at the shul. Or I might call Mr. Chinn."

"Mr. Chinn? Why?"

"He's rich, right? He must give a lot of *tzedakah*, right? Maybe he needs some help with coordinating or something."

Rivka wrinkled her forehead. "Doesn't he have secretaries?"

"Look, it's worth a try." Moishy lifted his finger up again, made a face, and put it down. He ate another pretzel.

"Don't you think your ideas are a little over-ambitious?" Rivka asked him.

Before he could answer, Yochie burst into the room. "You," she said, pointing to Moishy. "You! Get your finger off of that telephone!"

"Why?" Moishy asked innocently.

"Do you know how annoying it is to try to have a conversation when the line is constantly clicking?"

"If you wouldn't monopolize the telephone..."

"I just have to make a few calls!"

"A few." He held his wristwatch up so she could see it. "I won't tell you how long you've been on the phone..."

He let his finger slide off the button and held up the receiver. Instead of a dial tone, they could hear a voice saying clearly: "I'm on the phone!"

"Who is that?" Yochie ran out of the room.

Moishy sighed and hung up the telephone. Gathering up his pretzels, he said, "I guess I'll go and stand on line upstairs." Munching loudly, he left the room. Rivka echoed his sigh and followed him.

Up in the study Yochie was fuming and tapping her foot as Dini talked. When she hung up, Yochie and Chezky leapt for the telephone.

"Oh, no you don't," said Chezky holding down the receiver. "I was next in line."

"But I didn't finish," said Yochie.

"You left!" Chezky didn't move.

"Did anyone think to ask me if I'd finished?" said Dini

Tikva burst into the room. "I have to use the phone!"

"There's a line," Dini informed her. "You have to wait."

"But I have to call now," Tikva explained. "The woman at the Center for the Blind said to call her at exactly eight o'clock. That's the only time she's available." Tikva looked pleadingly at her brothers and sisters.

Chezky moved his hand off the telephone. "Go ahead," he said. No one objected.

Tikva talked for five minutes, telling the woman about herself and what she thought she could do. She hung up, her face glowing.

"She said she thought that she could use me," she told them. "I'm going down to the center tomorrow afternoon."

"Good!" said Dini. The others congratulated her. She floated out of the room. Dini reached for the telephone.

"I have just a few more phone calls to make!" said Yochie. The argument was on.

Ten minutes later Yochie, Moishy, and Chezky sat while Dini talked. Donny, in pajamas, lay on the floor, playing with one of his cars. He was supposed to be in bed, but no one wanted to risk losing his or her place in line to put him into bed. Zahava walked in.

"I have to use the phone..." Her voice trailed off. "You're waiting for the phone?" she asked Yochie.

"Yup."

"And you?" she asked Moishy.

"Yup."

"And you and you?" Chezky and Dini nodded. With a sigh, Zahava sat down.

"Did Tikki tell you about her job?" Yochie asked her.

"Yes," said Zahava, her face lighting up. "I think it's wonderful.

"She'll do a great job," said Yochie. "Girls are so good at *chesed*."

Moishy looked at her. "May I remind you that Avraham Avinu was not a girl?"

"That's why he was so remarkable," said Yochie.

Dini put her hand over the receiver. "Yochie!" she said in a loud whisper.

"Are you trying to say that you are more capable of doing *chesed* than us?" Moishy demanded.

"Not exactly," said Yochie, realizing that she'd overstepped her bounds. "It's just that girls have so many more opportunities..."

"I'll bet the Baker boys manage to do just as much *chesed* as the Baker girls, if not more!"

"That's right," said Chezky, banging one hand with the other fist.

"We're gonna do *oodles* of *chesed*!" said Donny, zooming his car across the floor.

Dini hung up the telephone. As Yochie went for her turn, she said, "We'll see."

After Yochie went Chezky, then Rivka, then Moishy, then Zahava. Then Yochie went again because she'd forgotten someone.

When she hung up, the phone rang. She picked it up and said, "Baker residence, can I help you?" After listening for a moment she covered the receiver with her hand. "It's for Abba."

"I'll get him!" Donny raced out of the room. He found his parents in the living room. Mr. Baker was sitting with a *sefer*, learning. Mrs. Baker lay on the couch with her feet up, eyes closed. "Telephone, Abba!" Donny sang out.

Mr. Baker put down his *sefer*. "That must be the phone call I was telling you about," he said to his wife. He looked up at the mantel clock. "It's much later than I expected it." He went out of the room. Donny started to follow him.

"Donny!" Donny stopped short. "Donny, what are you doing awake?"

"*Chesed!*" Donny promptly replied.

"Nice try, kid," said Mrs. Baker, and marched him up to bed.

Mr. Baker came into the study. He lifted an eyebrow in surprise when he saw how many children were there. "Hello?" he said into the phone.

"BAKER!" barked a voice on the other end. "I've been trying to call you all night!"

"Hello, Mr. Wein. How are you?" said Mr. Baker cheerfully.

"*Baruch Hashem*, fine!" the voice growled. The owner of the voice spoke so loudly that he could be heard clearly by everyone in the study. "What's wrong with your phone?"

"I don't know," said Mr. Baker a little uncertainly. He took the receiver from his ear and looked at it. "I'll check it out." He looked around the room. The children shifted uncomfortably.

"Baker, how's that Rachel girl?"

"The baby? Fine, Mr. Wein, fine, *baruch Hashem*."

"That's some cute kid, you got there, *keneina hara*. Bring her around again, you hear?"

"Certainly, Mr. Wein."

"Baker, I called to confirm our appointment. Ten o'clock is good. Okay?"

"Fine."

"Goodbye, Baker!"

"Goodbye, Mr. Wein." Mr. Baker hung up the telephone. The study was very quiet.

"Is everyone here?" he asked in a quiet voice.

"Donny was put to bed," said Rivka. "Um, I can go and get Tikki and Dini if you want."

"Do that." Rivka rushed out of the room. Mr. Baker picked up a *sefer*. The rest of the children sat nervously until Rivka returned with Tikva and Dini.

"Here we are," Rikva announced. Tikva and Dini could see that their father was upset about something but they couldn't imagine what.

Mr. Baker closed his *sefer*. "Thank you for being prompt. I would like to start with a question: What is our house rule about tying up the telephone?"

There was an awkward silence as the children struggled with their consciences. Finally, Dini cleared her throat and said, "We're supposed to keep it short, especially at night. We can have a long conversation or make several phone calls only with the permission of anyone else who might want to use the telephone."

"Right," said Mr. Baker in his courtroom voice. "Now can anyone tell me what went on here tonight?"

"But Abba," Yochie burst out. "It was for the *chesed* project."

"We had to make so many telephone calls to get things organized," Rivka joined in.

"It was for a mitzvah!" said Zahava, spreading her hands wide.

"A very important one," said Moishy, nodding his head sagely.

"*Zrizim makdimim l'mitzvos!*" said Chezky with one finger in the air. Everyone looked at him in surprise; Chezky usually didn't come up with anything useful in these kinds of conversations.

"And why didn't you come and discuss this with your mother and me?" Mr. Baker looked piercingly at them.

"We just assumed..."

"It seemed so obvious..."

"What else were we going to do?..."

"A mitzvah — it's a priority..." Everyone spoke at once.

Mr. Baker made an impatient gesture with his hand. The babble slowly faded. He looked at them and tapped his fingers on his leg.

"I think Ima and I made it clear that no one was to abandon any responsibilities for this project."

"Of course, Abba."

"Naturally."

"We understood that."

Mr. Baker hushed them again. "I hope that everyone will get their priorities straight."

"Straight priorities!"

"Of course."

"Don't worry, Abba."

"We've got our heads screwed on right."

"I guess that explains why you've all gone a little screwy," Mr. Baker muttered to himself.

"What?"

"Never mind. Do you have anything else to say?"

Silence. Zahava, Rivka, and Yochie all looked blank; Moishy was deep in thought. Chezky scratched his head, but it was more for effect than to help. Tikva looked at their father with a wrinkled brow. Finally, Dini ventured a timid "Sorry?"

"Forgiven!" said Mr. Baker, stepping briskly out of the study. "I suggest you kids start heading for bed now."

Yawning, Chezky decided to take his father's advice. He went to his room, where Donny was curled up asleep in his bed, the hall light shining on his face through the open door. Chezky remembered last night's nightmare, and hoped Donny — and the rest of the family — would enjoy an uninterrupted night this time. He yawned again, and quickly undressed and eased himself between the sheets. Aaah! he thought. Bed at last! I don't normally like to go to sleep, but some nights... Chezky snuggled under the covers. He said *krias Shema* slowly, enjoying each word. Then closed his eyes.

He was just drifting off when he felt a small warm body snuggle up next to him.

"Donny?" Chezky mumbled sleepily.

No answer. Chezky half-sat up and looked over his shoulder. It was Donny, curled up in a ball.

"Donny," Chezky whispered."Donny?" No answer.

Chezky looked at his small brother for a moment. In the light from the night-light in the hall he looked younger than his age and vulnerable. Sighing, Chezky pushed himself into the wall in order to make more room. He was so tired that in seconds — right in the middle of another enormous yawn — he was fast asleep.

Meanwhile, outside the study, Mr. Baker stopped to loosen his tie. He reviewed the night's events in his mind as he walked down the hall. "Storm clouds ahead," he said to himself. "I suspect this is a 'learn it the hard way' situation." He started down the hall. "I just hope that it won't be too hard on those of us who don't need to learn it."

Mr. Baker went down to the kitchen where he found his wife making the sandwiches for the next day. Quickly, he told her about his talk with the children. She was about to reply when the phone rang.

"Just don't let it be Mr. Wein." Mr. Baker winced as it rang again. Mrs. Baker picked it up.

"Hello? One moment. I'll see if she's still awake." Putting her hand over the receiver, she whispered to her husband, "It's for Bracha."

Mr. Baker sighed. "I'll go get her."

"It's alright. I'll go." Mrs. Baker put the receiver down on the counter and went upstairs. She found Bracha in her room holding her pajamas, and realized she was almost ready for bed.

"Bracha, there's a phone call for you. You know I don't like schoolfriends calling so late, but I'll make an exception this time; I know that the line was tied up all night. It's someone named Naomi, and she says it's important."

Mrs. Baker could see Bracha go through an inner struggle. "Could I bother you to tell her that I can't come to the phone," she asked finally. "I'm nearly in bed, and I'm too tired. I'll see her in the morning."

Mrs. Baker studied her daughter. "Alright, Bracha," she said. "Goodnight."

Mrs. Baker went down to the kitchen, gave the message to Bracha's friend, and hung up.

"That was so strange," she said to her husband. "Here is everyone going '*chesed* crazy,' and there's Bracha refusing to talk to someone who seems to need her..."

5
First Day on the Job

In the end, Rivka settled on tutoring," said Mrs. Baker. She was sitting in the kitchen enjoying a cup of coffee. Mr. Baker had come in from his office in the garden and, on the spur of the moment, had decided to join her. They'd put some frozen cake in the microwave and were now enjoying a small feast.

"I thought she had her heart set on being a mother's helper," said Mr. Baker, helping himself to a piece of cake.

"She did, but it seems that there aren't enough mothers to go around."

Mr. Baker smiled. "I'll bet all of those mothers are wondering what this is all about."

"And wondering how long it will last," Mrs. Baker quipped. "After Lag Ba'Omer I think that it will be back to 'Help, I need a babysitter!' " She sipped her coffee.

Mr. Baker nodded in agreement and laughed. "What about the others? Did Tikki get the job she wanted?"

"Yes," Mrs. Baker smiled happily. "She'll be doing at least three hours a week at the Center for the Blind."

"Terrific! It will be good for her and good for them." Mr. Baker reached for another piece of cake.

"Zahava and Yochie are going to be mother's helpers," Mrs. Baker continued.

"I suppose the mother isn't you, is it?"

"Ephraim, you know I don't need help!" Mrs. Baker joked.

Her husband snorted.

"Besides," she said, "Donny has decided that his *chesed* project will be babysitting for Saraleh in the afternoons so I can get some extra work done."

"Why is it that only the six-year-old gets the hint?" Mr. Baker rolled his eyes to the ceiling.

"Dini will be working for *Tomchei Shabbos*, packing up food boxes."

Mr. Baker nodded and sipped his coffee. He eyed the plate of cake. Donny wandered into the kitchen.

"Hi, Donny," said his mother. Mr. Baker smiled at him.

"Hi." He climbed onto a chair. "Can I have cake?"

"Sure." Mrs. Baker gave him a piece. His father watched him thoughtfully.

"Moishy is going to help Great-Aunt Frieda, and Chezky is going to Mr. Schwartz," Mrs. Baker continued.

"What happened to all of Moishy's grand ideas?"

"He was surprised that Mr. Chinn didn't need his help," said Mrs. Baker, eyes twinkling. "But he said Mr. Chinn was very polite on the phone."

"I'll bet he was," Mr. Baker chuckled. "Good old Chinn. What's happening with your outings with the kids?"

"I'm taking Zahava out this afternoon. We'll see how it goes." Mrs. Baker cleared the table.

"Ima, I want to go out with you too!" Donny said through a mouth full of crumbs.

"What?"

"I'm big. I want a day just with you too!"

"But you spend most afternoons with me." Mrs. Baker looked at her son with loving eyes.

"Not alo-one." Donny finished his cake and wiped his mouth on his sleeve.

Mrs. Baker was taken aback. "Donny boy, you're full of surprises." She reached over to him and adjusted his *kippah*. "I'll think about it."

"Well, I think I'll get back to work." Mr. Baker went to the back door. Suddenly, he turned around. "I thought there weren't any babysitting jobs available. How did Yochie and Zahava luck out?"

"They got to the phone first."

The building that housed the Center for the Blind was made of warm red brick. It had a small front garden dominated by two large maple trees; the maple trees were surrounded with early flowers. Over the front door, which had a brass knocker, was a huge black and white sign that said, "The Mark Goodman Center for the Blind." Tikva wondered who Mark Goodman was.

Swallowing down the butterflies in her stomach, she grasped the big, brass knocker and tapped it on the door. It made a hollow-sounding boom that seemed to echo deep inside the building. After a minute, she heard someone coming. The door opened.

"Hello!" Tikva recognized the voice of the woman she'd spoken to on the phone. "You must be Tikva Baker."

"Yes, I am. Are you Miss. Katz?" Tikva asked.

"Yes, I am. Please come in." They walked through a small entranceway into a brightly lit hall. The walls were yellow and decorated with colorful abstract paintings.

"Would you like to look around a bit?"

"Yes, please," said Tikva eagerly. The Center for the Blind was recently established, and she had never been inside.

"We'll start at the back and work our way to the front," said Miss Katz as she led Tikva down the hall. "We like to think of the Mark Goodman Center for the Blind as a kind of community center with an extra purpose," she explained as they went. "We have many courses and activities for the visually impaired."

Tikva liked her voice. She felt it had a smile in it.

"We are here to help the person who is not as independent as he would like to be, a person who wants to learn more skills for coping."

"Oh, that's good," said Tikva.

"The people who come here are all ages and kinds. Some are visually impaired from birth; most are not. They come here to help themselves find the skills to adjust to their new lifestyle, and to find people who can give them understanding and support." Miss Katz put her hand on a door and turned to Tikva.

"I just want to say I think it's wonderful that you came to volunteer here. Not many eleven-year-olds would think of it."

Tikva blushed. "I'm nearly twelve, actually. And to tell the truth, I didn't think of it myself," she confessed. "It's a class project."

"A class project?"

"Yes," she said. "Everyone in the class must pick out a *ches*...a...a kind act. A good deed." Tikva felt flustered. "After a few weeks, each person will give a report on what they've been doing and what they learned."

"That's some project!" said Miss Katz. "I'm very impressed!" They looked at the kitchen, where cooking classes took place and food was prepared for parties and other events. Then they saw the library with its large selection of Braille books and audio tapes, rooms for arts and crafts, computers, the office and, last of all, a large and comfortable sitting room.

"This is our social hall," Miss Katz explained. "Here people come to sit and relax, and socialize. Some times we have events here, like a small concert. People often come here between activities."

Tikva nodded. "What is the upstairs used for?"

"A preschool."

"Where do your preschoolers go when they finish here?" Tikva asked.

"Most of our pupils go on to special schools," Miss Katz replied. "But some go into the regular school system. In the afternoon we have a day-care center for small children whose parents work."

Another woman put her head in the door. "Miss Katz, phone call for you," she called.

"Thanks, Marge." Miss Katz turned to Tikva. "I won't be long. Would you like to wait here? We have some magazines..."

"That's fine." Tikva watched Miss Katz leave the room.

When she was gone, Tikva examined the room. It was decorated in bright colors, something appreciated by a person who had some vision. There were large sofas and soft chairs. The floor was covered with a soft rug. Small tables were put at the sides of the couches, making sure that there were no obstructions for sight-impaired people to trip on.

"*Lifnei iver lo sitein michshol*," she thought to herself, and sat down on a sofa.

Tikva picked up one of the magazines and ran her fingertips over the pages, but her mind wasn't on reading. She thought about her own experiences as a girl whose sight was so limited, and how difficult it had been to gain acceptance in school — and in the world — as a "normal" girl.

And now here I am, trying to help other people like me. I've been thinking about doing something like this for a while, but the class project made it happen. I want to help all of the people I meet, but especially if I happen to meet a little girl...

"Tikva?" Tikva looked up to find Miss Katz standing over her. Her phone call was finished.

"Sorry about that," she smiled. "Now, let's talk about what you'll be doing..."

Somehow, some hairs had slipped out of her ponytail and fallen into her face. Dini pushed them out of her eyes and picked up another can. Never in her life, outside of the supermarket, had she seen so much food at once! When she'd walked into the room, she thought they'd never get it packed. Now she was sure.

"Pass me the tape dispenser, please." Dini looked around behind her and picked up the tape dispenser. She passed it to the woman next to her.

"Thank you!"

Not only am I the youngest person here, Dini thought, but I'll bet everyone is at least twice as old as me, if not three or four times older. I wish that Idy's aunt hadn't broken her leg. Then Idy would be here with me. Instead, Idy is helping her, and I'm all alone. She picked up two more cans and put them in a box.

"Teatime!" sang out one of the women. She went over to an enormous bag and pulled out a large thermos and a pile of styrofoam cups. After she poured tea for one or two women, she came over to Dini.

"Would you like some tea, dear?" Dini looked at the woman, who seemed old enough to be her grandmother, and decided that it was alright for her to call her "dear."

"Yes, please," Dini replied.

"It's hard work, packing these boxes," the woman continued. "It looks so easy, but after the five hundredth can, your arms begin to get tired."

Several women chuckled as Dini nodded in agreement. "Where are these boxes headed?" she asked.

"To Russia, eventually," the woman told her. "Some will stay here in the U.S.A."

"Last year we went to Russia," another woman said. Dini recognized her as a woman who sometimes davened at their shul, Mrs. Lederman. Her husband was known to be a great *talmid chacham*. "We stayed for three months, teaching at a summer yeshiva. You can't imagine the hunger there, shortages and low wages. No one starves, but they get pretty hungry, especially if they keep kosher. When boxes like these showed up, people were very grateful."

The other women murmured in wonder and agreement.

"There are many cases in the U.S. too," said another woman. "Here in Bloomfield we are very lucky. Although you'd be surprised."

"It's true — some of our boxes stay right here," Mrs. Lederman said.

"Here in Bloomfield?" Dini blurted out.

Mrs. Lederman smiled at her, a sad smile. "Yes, dear," she said, and went back to her packing.

There are poor people here? Dini stirred uncomfortably and looked around as if she expected them to come streaming through the door. Who could they be? No one in Bloomfield looked poor.

Could there be any poor people in my class? Dini thought about a girl in her class who always wore the most out-of-date things. The girl's sister's did, too. Were they poor?

This same girl often didn't come to special functions; she said it was because she had to babysit for her little brothers. Maybe she really didn't have the money?

Dini tried to imagine what it must be like to be hungry and found that it wasn't so easy. She thought of the feeling when dinner was late, but decided that that didn't count, because she knew that dinner was coming soon. What about those days when she was almost late for school, and she skipped breakfast. How she longed for lunch all morning. And what if lunch never came, or only a very tiny one?

Dini picked up two more cans and packed them in another box. She worked faster now and didn't look up at the clock. What could I do if that girl in my class really is poor? Should I take her and her sister out sometime? Maybe treat them to pizza or something?

Dini packed her last two cans. She noticed that there were many full boxes, and so she went up to Mrs. Lederman, who was in charge.

"Excuse me, should I tape up those boxes?" she asked.

"Which ones?" asked the woman, craning her neck to see over other packers. "Yes, that's a good idea. There's the dispenser," she added, pointing to a table. She turned and smiled at Dini. "Good for you that you think for yourself and look to see what needs to be done. I wish we had more volunteers like you!"

Dini blushed with pleasure and went to tape up the boxes.

It was nice of Mrs. Lederman to say that, she thought. Now, about that poor girl. I could easily invite her to a concert. I could pay for the tickets out of my allowance if I'm careful...

Dini stopped pulling at the tape dispenser and frowned. Something was bothering her, and she thought she knew what it was. She turned to the woman next to her and asked, "Do these people know who's giving them the boxes? Can we know who they're going to?"

"The people who receive the boxes only know that they're from a particular organization," said the woman. "They don't really know who works here. And, except for Mrs. Lederman, no one knows who they go to. It's best to keep it a secret as much as possible."

A secret, Dini thought. Why? So the person won't be embarrassed, of course. Imagine if I saw the poor woman in shul, and I came up to her and asked how she liked the food. She'd be very embarrassed.

Dini pushed herself to work faster as she thought. If I start treating that girl and she can't treat me back, she'll be embarrassed. She might not want to go with me. Plus she'll know that I know she has no money. I'll have to think of something else.

"Dini, darling?"

Dini looked up into the kind eyes of Mrs. Lederman. They were very dark, almost black. Those eyes could keep secrets, Dini thought. Lots of secrets. I'd trust those eyes if I was in trouble.

"Dini, we're done for the day; two hours is enough," Mrs. Lederman chuckled gently. "You were so busy that you didn't even notice we were stopping." Mrs. Lederman smiled at her. "Thank you for coming; you worked so well."

"You were wonderful," said another woman.

"I wish my daughter was like that," a third exclaimed.

"Not many young people understand the importance of what we do here," Mrs. Lederman continued. "Some people can't imagine what it's like to be really hungry. You meet someone in the grocery, in shul — they look fine. You don't know what they've been through. They could be starving and still smile." Dini noticed that Mrs. Lederman had a slight accent. It's funny I never noticed that before, she thought. I guess I've never really spoken to her.

Mrs. Lederman smiled at her again and gently pinched her cheek. "You're coming again?" she asked.

"Yes," said Dini, with much feeling.

"Good."

One by one the women left, but Dini lingered. She had a lot to think about. When she finally left, she walked home slowly.

"Okay, Natalia, are you ready?" Rivka looked down at the second-grader's heart-shaped face and smiled.

"Yes, ready." Natalia spoke softly, with a heavy accent. Her family had come from the Ukraine at the beginning of the school year. She worked very hard, but she needed help to keep up.

"Good!" Rivka smoothed down the pages of the easy reader that she'd brought with her and pointed to the first line. "Go ahead and read."

Natalia looked at the page and didn't say a word.

"Go ahead, Natalia, I'm listening." Rivka smiled as encouragingly as she could.

Natalia just looked.

Rivka smoothed the page and looked at her pupil. "Natalia, is there something wrong?"

Natalia looked up at her and smiled shyly. She didn't say a word.

What could be the problem? Rivka wondered. Maybe she doesn't like the book? "Don't you want to read the book?" she asked.

Natalia nodded.

"So go ahead and read!"

Natalia smiled at her again.

"It's really a nice book," Rivka tried to persuade her. "And the pictures are so lovely. Don't you want to know the story?"

Natalia nodded.

Rivka smoothed her hand over the book again and pointed to the page. What's wrong with this kid? "Come, I'll help you. The first word is a name..."

"Your hand is over words," said Natalia in a whisper.

"What?"

Natalia pointed to Rivka's hand that rested on the left page. "Your hand is over words."

Rivka picked up her left hand. Underneath were the tiny words that told about the copyright and Library of Congress numbers.

"Oh, Natalia, you don't have to read that!" Rivka couldn't believe this was happening. Didn't Natalia know anything about books?

"I like to read everything." Natalia looked up at her with big, dark eyes.

"But it's not even part of the story!"

"I know. I like read it all." Natalia put out her lower lip.

Rivka sighed. "Go ahead."

Natalia put her index finger next to the first word. "First pub...pub..." She looked up at Rivka. "What is word?"

"Published."

"First published 1991," Natalia read. "Copy...copyright 1991 by Sefer Press. Isbin?"

"No. It's initials," Rivka explained. "You read it I.S.B.N."

"I.S.B.N. Zero, nine five seven seven seven zero, six three ex. All rights reserved." Natalia moved her finger to the next line.

"We really don't have to read all this," Rivka tried again. "It such a nice story, all about...all about..." Rivka's voice trailed off as she saw Natalia staring at her. "Go ahead," she sighed.

Rivka followed along as she found out that no part of this publication may be translated, etc., etc., and who published it, and who distributed it. And where it was printed. She helped Natalia through several hard words. When they finished the page Rivka looked at her watch.

"There's only ten minutes left!" she exclaimed. "We spent most of the time on nothing!"

"I no understand," said Natalia, looking at Rivka with her level stare. "We read, no?"

The door was opened by an overdressed little girl about six years old. She took one look at Yochie and slammed it shut again. Surprised, Yochie waited a minute and rang again. This time the door was opened by a boy, a little younger, dressed in an outfit Donny would have worn for Shabbos. Maybe his mother is taking him with her, Yochie thought.

"What do you want?" the boy asked.

"I'm Yochie," said Yochie, wearing her brightest smile. "Your mother's expecting me."

The boy stared at her for a moment, then slammed the door.

Undaunted, Yochie rang the doorbell, leaning into it for a good, long ring.

"Who is it?" sang an adult woman's voice from inside the house.

"Yochie Baker."

The door opened. Standing there was a tall woman, dressed in black. She wore a high, severely waved *sheitel*, large gold earrings, and several lengths of gold chain around her neck. Her face was very heavily made up, and her fingers were covered with large rings. She looked Yochie up and down, and sniffed.

"You must learn to be more patient," she said. "A woman with children cannot always come to the door right away. Next time, ring once and wait."

Yochie opened her mouth to defend herself, but before she could explain Mrs. Freulich swept her into the house.

What a house! Yochie thought. Down the long hall was a stretch of luxurious carpet covered in the middle by a plastic runway. To her left, Yochie caught a glimpse of a vast living room, with display cabinets and small tables full of knick-knacks. All the furniture was covered with plastic slipcovers. Mrs. Freulich led her down the hall, speaking rapidly.

"I'm really glad you could come. I must go out every week at this time, and I was desperate for some help. The children are darlings. I'm sure you'll have no problems with them..."

Yochie, after her experience at the door, was not so sure. As she heard the mother speak, she began to wonder why her friend told her that it was a real *chesed* to help this family. She sounded like she had everything under control.

"You may play with them until suppertime, which is exactly at five o'clock. They may not play anywhere but the playroom or the garden, and in the garden they may only play on the grass. They may color in the kitchen, but only on the table and the table must be covered with newspaper. Only one game at a time, and they must all share. After I leave they can have their snack, which is laid out in the kitchen. Each child must sit on his or her own chair and wear an apron. No spilling and no blowing bubbles in their milk. My big girl, Mashie, must do her homework. The other children may work in their workbooks, but only one page, and it must be finished. Don't do Mashie's homework for her, but she really does need help..." Mrs. Freulich went on, but Yochie got lost in the sea of instructions. They came to the end of the hall and went into the kitchen.

The kitchen was huge, modern, and spotlessly clean. Four children sat at the table. Silent and wary, they stared at Yochie.

"This is Yochie, *kinderlach*!" said Mrs. Freulich in a musical voice.

"Hi, kids," said Yochie. The children did not reply.

"They're a little shy," said Mrs. Freulich quickly. "The biggest is Mashie. She's six. Berel is five, Raizel is four, and Kalman is three." She looked at her watch. "*Oy*, I must run." She kissed each child on the head. "Be good, *kinderlach*!" Yochie wondered if there wasn't a kind of desperation in her voice. It must be my imagination, she thought. The children stared at her.

"Don't go," said the biggest.

"I have to, *mammaleh*, you know that. Goodbye. I won't be too long, I hope!" She ran out the back door. It slammed shut behind her.

Yochie turned to the children. "Why didn't you say goodbye to your mother?" she asked.

The children kept on staring at her. "We don't like you," said Mashie at last.

"Why, why not?" Yochie stammered.

"We don't like babysitters," said Kalman.

"That's not nice!" Berel yelled. He hit his brother on the head.

"Hey!" said Yochie, jumping forward. Kalman hit Berel back, and within a second they were having a fistfight.

"Stop!" Yochie cried as she pried them apart. "No hitting!"

"He started it!" screeched Kalman as he struggled to get at his brother. Berel stuck out his tongue. Kalman struggled harder. "I'll bash you! I'll bash you!" he cried. Yochie dragged him over to the other side of the kitchen and told him to stay there.

"I'm bored," Mashie announced.

Yochie stood in front of Kalman. She was slightly out of breath. "Why don't you get your homework?" she suggested.

"I'll get the workbooks!" Berel went to a large drawer in another corner of the kitchen and began to dump its contents on the floor.

"Berel!" Yochie was horrified. She didn't want Mrs. Freulich to come home and find her beautiful kitchen a wreck. She ran over and began stuffing papers and books back in the drawer.

"How can I find anything?" Berel demanded, and began to dump out the drawer again.

Meanwhile, Mashie brought her book bag into the kitchen and went out again. Raizel, who up until now had been sitting on her chair and sucking her thumb, went over to the book bag. By the time Yochie finally noticed what she was doing, she'd carefully colored all over her sister's math book with a red crayon.

"Raizel!" Yochie rushed over and grabbed the crayon out of her hand. Mashie came back, took one look at her math book, and began to wail. She picked up the box of crayons and threw it at Raizel.

"No!" Yochie caught the box just before it hit Raizel in the face. Quickly she gathered up the contents of Mashie's book bag and dumped them on the table. "Just sit here and get organized. Raizel, that wasn't nice. Don't cry, Mashie, we'll fix it up somehow."

Berel came over with workbooks and began to work on one.

"Your mother said only one page," Yochie reminded him.

"I know."

Yochie set Raizel up with another workbook and looked around for Kalman. He wasn't in the corner where she'd left him. However, the refrigerator door was open, and two small legs were sticking out from under it.

"Kalman, what are you doing?"

"Eating."

Yochie hurried over to the refrigerator. There was Kalman, eating something out of a large box.

Yochie smelled it. "That's chopped liver!" She read the words on the lid, which Kalman had thrown on the floor. "From New York! That's incredibly expensive!"

"I like it," said Kalman, taking another handful.

Yochie took the box from him and closed the refrigerator door. She was taking him over to the sink to wash his hands when she heard a shriek from the table. Mashie was pulling Raizel's hair. She dropped Kalman and rushed over to the table. As she passed the clock over the sinks she saw, with a sinking heart, that only seven minutes of her two hours had passed. How am I going to last the afternoon? she wondered in despair. There's only one thing I don't wonder any more, she thought as she struggled to separate the two fighting children. I don't wonder why my friend said that helping out here is such a mitzvah.

6

Dogs, Sweets, and Serenades

We won't have a lot of time today, Chezky, because I have to take Charley to the veterinarian."

"Is he sick?" Chezky patted the big dog on his head as he listened to Mr. Schwartz. Charley smiled a doggy smile and wagged his tail.

"No, he's not sick. It's time for his annual checkup." Mr. Schwartz shifted his hold on the rake in his hand and patted the dog too. Charley looked from Chezky to his master and back again, and wagged his tail harder.

"I didn't know that dogs needed checkups!" Chezky tried to imagine a doctor in a white coat listening to Charley's heart with a stethoscope.

"Oh yes, they do," said Mr. Schwartz. "Just like us. Come, let's get to work." He shouldered the rake and walked across the garden. Chezky followed, lugging gardening equipment and garbage bags.

"In the spring," Mr. Schwartz explained as he walked, "there's a lot of work to do in a garden. Everything has to be gotten ready to grow."

"That's right," Chezky agreed.

"The hardest work is getting rid of the thatch in the grass."

"Thatch?"

"That's the old dried grass from last year," Mr. Schwartz explained. "It covers the ground so the new grass can't get through.'

"Oh, that stuff," said Chezky. "My Abba has a gardener come in and do it."

"So do I. But he doesn't get to every corner. To save money, I do some of it myself." Mr. Schwartz put down his rake and pointed to a patch of grass under a tree. "Look here." Chezky looked where he pointed. "Under the tree is the roots. The machine couldn't work here." Mr. Schwartz smiled fondly. "I like the grass to be green, and this here, it's one of my favorite places to sit in the summer. My grandchildren like it here too, when they come to visit. Put down all that stuff, and I'll show you what we have to do."

Chezky dropped everything that was in his hands. A large shovel bumped into the watering can and fell over sideways, right onto Charley's paw. He yelped and sped to the other side of the garden.

"Oh, Charley, I'm sorry!" Chezky whistled for the big dog, who came limping back. Mr. Schwartz bent down and examined the paw.

"It looks alright," he said. "Just a bruise." Pointing to another tree, he told Charley to go sit. Charley did so, still limping.

"I'm so sorry," Chezky apologized again. "I'll try and be more careful. You could show it to the doctor this afternoon," he added.

"Don't worry about it, Chezky." Mr. Schwartz took up the rake. "Now watch what I do." Chezky watched as Mr. Schwartz began hacking away at the grass, removing all the old, dried-up blades between the new growth. Soon he was puffing and panting with the effort.

"Mr. Schwartz," said Chezky, worried that the older man might exert himself too much, "I get it now. I'll do it."

Mr. Schwartz straightened up and wiped his brow. "Okay," he panted. "Here." He handed the rake to Chezky who began hacking away at the grass. Mr. Schwartz looked on, smiling.

Chezky raked and dug, enjoying the exercise and feeling good about helping Mr. Schwartz. He raked more and more enthusiastically, moving backwards as he finished with a patch.

"Easy does it," called Mr. Schwartz, beginning to be concerned, but it was too late. Chezky lowered his rake in order to raise it high again, and the handle caught on the watering can behind him. The can flew in the air right towards Mr. Schwartz, who grabbed his head and ducked just in time.

Chezky stared at Mr. Schwartz, amazed and thankful that his head was still on his shoulders.

Slowly, the old man straightened up and took his hands off his head.

"Wow, Mr. Schwartz, I sure am sorry!" said Chezky. "*Baruch Hashem*, it didn't hit your head!"

"*Baruch Hashem*." Mr. Schwartz rubbed his head as if to make sure it was still there. "I'm, um, going to work in the vegetable garden for awhile. I'll be back soon."

"Okay!" Chezky was already raking again.

Chezky raked and dug. Look at all that stuff come away! The grass sure is going to have a lot of room to grow here.

When Charley saw his master go to the other side of the garden, he stood up and stretched. Slowly he sauntered over to Chezky and sniffed at the newly exposed dirt.

"Hi, Charley!" Chezky smiled at the big, black dog as he dug. Charley looked up and wagged his tail. Then he sniffed at the ground again and scraped at it with his paw.

"Do you want to dig too, boy?" Chezky asked him.

As if he understood, Charley began to dig with his front feet. Faster and faster he dug, until the dirt was flying.

"Go, Charley, go!" Chezky cried as he laid to with his rake. Charley barked and kept digging.

"Stop!" Chezky and Charley turned at the sound of the voice. There was Mr. Schwartz, looking a little frazzled.

"Er, um, uh, quite a job you're doing there, boys," he stammered.

"Charley is some digger!" Chezky scratched the big dog behind the ears.

"He sure is..." Mr. Schwartz rubbed the back of his neck a few times, and stared at the pit in his lawn. "I think I have another job for you — in the vegetable garden."

"Okay, Mr. Schwartz!" Chezky dropped his rake and started across the lawn.

Mr. Schwartz picked up the rake and looked at the patch Chezky and Charley had cleared. Then he leaned the rake against the tree and took out a small pad, where he wrote: "Buy grass seed." Sighing, he walked across the lawn, Charley trotting behind him.

"What are we going to do here, Mr. Schwartz?" Chezky asked him when he arrived.

"There are a couple of early vegetables that need thinning." Mr. Schwartz pointed to a few long furrows, each dotted with tiny, green plants.

"Great!"

"Do you know how to thin?" Mr. Schwartz asked him.

"Yep!"

Mr. Schwartz looked uneasily across the garden. "You can start with the carrots." He pointed to the row closest to them. "I'll be setting out tomato plants if you want me."

"Okay, Mr. Schwartz." Chezky got down on his hands and knees next to the row of carrots. Mr. Schwartz picked up a box of young tomato plants and went to the opposite corner of the vegetable patch.

Chezky put his hand on the first plant. Charley came over to investigate. "You see, Charley, the important thing is to know what to thin," he explained. "If you don't do it right, then the plants won't grow nicely." Charley gave a small whuff and looked at Chezky and back at the carrot sprouts.

"Ima showed me on the house plants," he continued. "First you pinch the leaves on the top. That will make the plant grow bushy. Then you look for any dead leaves or scraggly branches. You pinch these off so the plant will have a nice shape." Charley blinked.

"These are very tiny plants, Charley." Chezky carefully pinched of the top of the first carrot plant. "And they must be very healthy; there aren't any dead leaves." Chezky worked his way down the row, Charley following.

When he go to the end of the row, there was Mr. Schwartz. "Chezky, what are you doing?"

"Thinning, like my mother taught me." Chezky demonstrated on the last plant. "You see, first you pinch the top so the plant will grow bushy..."

"That's...that's fine, Chezky, my boy," Mr. Schwartz was staring down the row of carrot plants, each one a little shorter than it was before. "You say that your mother taught you this in the garden?"

"My mother doesn't let me work in the garden, much," Chezky told him. "She says that Bracha helps her a lot and she doesn't need me. I learned this on the house plants."

"I see." Mr. Schwartz looked down the row of carrot plants. Sighing, he took out his little pad and wrote:

"Buy carrot seeds." Then he turned to Chezky. "Why don't you take Charley for a little walk?" he suggested.

"Okay." Chezky whistled for Charley. "Let's go walk, boy." Chezky went to get the leash that hung on the back porch. He turned to say goodbye to Mr. Schwartz and saw him kneeling down by the carrots. "I guess he liked our work, boy," he said to the dog. Charley wagged his tail. "Goodbye, Mr. Schwartz!" Chezky called, and broke into a run.

Mr. Schwartz looked up from his examination of the carrots. "Don't forget Charley has an appointment at the vet!" he called after them as they jumped over the garden gate. "*Oy*, that kid!" he said softly. "I hope he heard me." He looked down the row of carrots once more, shook his head, and started gathering up the gardening things.

Chezky ran down the block with Charley trotting easily beside him. Chezky admired the dog's big muscles and easy movements. "I'll bet you could really run, boy," he said. "I'll bet I couldn't run faster than you." Chezky ran a little faster, Charley trotted along beside him. He ran faster still, and Charley broke into a lope. It didn't even look like an effort for him. Chezky ran as fast as he could. The two of them sped down the block.

The gardening things were put away, and the house was locked up. Mr. Schwartz looked at his watch. I have to leave soon, he thought. Standing at the gate, he peered down the block. Where could they be? He looked at his watch and searched in the other direction, shading his eyes from the sun. "*Oy, yoy, yoy,*

yoy," he sighed. "Now I'm gonna have to take the car to get there in time." He went to the garage and backed out his ancient Ford. Once in the street he looked around again. *"Vey, vey, vey,"* he muttered. He got out of the car so he could see farther.

What was that in the distance? Why were they running so fast? Mr. Schwartz jumped into the car and gunned the engine. Just as he was ready to drive, Chezky and Charley thudded to a halt. Chezky collapsed against the car, breathing heavily.

"Boy, can he run, Mr. Schwartz!" Chezky looked admiringly at Charley, who was hardly panting. "I ran my fastest, and he practically walked! Well, not really, but it wasn't hard for him. Why are you in the car? Oh, the animal doctor." Chezky opened the back door and Charley jumped in.

"It was great helping you, Mr. Schwartz." Chezky spoke more clearly as he began to catch his breath. "I love doing *chesed.*"

Mr. Schwartz opened his mouth to say something, but Chezky kept going. "We got so much done today in the garden, it was incredible. And I walked Charley for you too! What a great day!"

Mr. Schwartz nodded weakly.

"I can hardly wait to come back. I'll help you out again, okay?" Chezky smiled at Mr. Schwartz, his face glowing.

Mr. Schwartz turned away and put his car into gear. "Er, aaah, I'm sure a, uh, helpful boy like you is very busy," he said.

"Naaaah!" Chezky assured him. "For you I always have time."

Mr. Schwartz looked at Chezky again. He'd stopped panting by now and was leaning against the window. His cheeks were flushed, his hair tousled, his shoelaces untied, and he grinned from ear to ear. "Listen, Chezky, I gotta go..."

"I'll see you tomorrow?"

"No, no, not tomorrow!" Mr. Schwartz cried. Chezky's face fell. "Not tomorrow.... Uh, the next day. Is that good for you?" He reached over and patted Chezky's hand.

Chezky's face brightened. "Sure, Mr. Schwartz, great!" He grabbed Mr. Schwartz's hand, shook it, and backed away from the car, waving.

"What could I do?" Mr. Schwartz said softly as he wound up the window. "That kid has such a face."

"Should I do the dishes, Great-Aunt Frieda?" Moishy asked.

"No, darling, they're done."

"Should I sweep the kitchen?"

"No, darling, I did that already."

Moishy sat for a minute and thought. "Do you want me to polish your silver?"

"No *ziskeit*, I do it every *motza'ei Shabbos*." Great-Aunt Frieda looked up from her knitting and smiled.

"How about the garden? Is there something I can do in the garden?" Moishy was beginning to feel desperate.

"No, *yingeleh*. My Yankel came on Sunday and took care of everything." She stopped knitting and counted stitches. Satisfied, she went on.

"Isn't there anything I can do for you?"

Great-Aunt Frieda put her knitting down and thought. "Do you know how to wind wool into a ball?"

"What?"

"Come, I'll show you." She took a large skein of wool out of her knitting bag. "You wind it around your hand like this, a lot of times. Then you take it off and wind it again, the other way. You keep doing this until the wool is finished. Do you understand?"

"No problem." Moishy wound three balls of wool. It took him five minutes.

"Beautiful!" said Great-Aunt Frieda, looking up from her knitting when he was done. "Such lovely balls of wool. It's so much easier to knit with good balls; they don't tangle." She put the balls of wool in her bag and went back to her knitting.

"Is there anything else I can do for you?"

"Just having you here is such a pleasure." Great-Aunt Frieda smiled at him.

But it's not a very big *chesed*, Moishy thought. Terrific, just terrific! Tikva is teaching the blind, Dini is giving food to the poor, Rivka is teaching the entire Russian population of Bloomfield, Yochie is helping thousands of mothers, Chezky is helping an old man, and I wind three balls of wool. Moishy kicked at his chair.

Great-Aunt Frieda looked up. "Is everything alright, Moishy? Maybe you're hungry. I'll get you a little snack." She put down her knitting and went into the kitchen.

"No, no, it's okay!" Moishy cried.

"It's no bother," Great-Aunt Frieda called from the kitchen.

Moishy ran into the kitchen "I'll get it! Really, Great-Aunt Frieda, don't!"

"I told you it's no bother. You're my guest." She took out a huge yeast cake and cut. "Go inside and sit down; I'm coming."

Great, thought Moishy. Not only am I not doing any *chesed* for Great-Aunt Frieda — she's doing *chesed* for me! Moishy went back to the sofa and sat down.

Great-Aunt Frieda soon followed with a tray containing a plate of cake, a bowl of fruit, a pot of tea, lemon juice, a sugar bowl, and two cups.

"I thought I'd join you," she said as she poured the tea.

Moishy grinned at her. Great-Aunt Frieda always gave you tea, no matter how old you were, and she never let you eat alone. Moishy made a *brachah* and bit into the cake.

"This is terrific!" he said sincerely. Great-Aunt Frieda was a great cook.

"Thank you, *ziskeit*," She took up her knitting again and ate between rows.

Moishy sipped his tea and thought. This is delicious cake, but it doesn't solve my problem. He looked around the room; his eyes stopped on the pictures above the mantel. The largest picture was of Great-Uncle Feivel, who died before Moishy was born. Great-

Aunt Frieda is an *almanah*, a widow, Moishy thought to himself. A person should be kind to an *almanah*; they're lonely, for one thing. Maybe she needs cheering up...

"Great-Aunt Frieda!" he said suddenly.

Great-Aunt Frieda jumped and dropped a stitch. "What is it Moishy?" she said as she looked for a crochet hook to help her recover the dropped stitch.

"I'm in a choir," Moishy announced.

"Is that so?" Great-Aunt Frieda held her knitting close to her eyes and maneuvered the crochet hook between the stitches.

"I can sing for you." Moishy smiled, showing all of his teeth.

Great-Aunt Frieda carefully maneuvered the stitch back onto one of her knitting needles. "That's a nice idea, dear," she said absently.

Moishy took a big swallow of tea to clear his throat. What shall I sing first? he wondered. I know!

"*Ivdu es Hashem besimchah, ivdu es Hashem besimchah!*" he sang.

Great-Aunt Frieda looked up from her knitting, startled. After considering Moishy for a moment or two, she put her crochet hook in her bag and went back to her knitting.

When Moishy finished, she dropped her work and applauded. "Oh, Moishy, that was so wonderful! What a voice you have, like a *chazzan!*" Moishy bowed and started his next song. For some reason, Great-Aunt Frieda looked slightly alarmed. Slowly, she picked up her knitting again.

Moishy chose the medley that the choir was doing for their Lag Ba'Omer concert. Since he thought that his great-aunt would enjoy it, he sang each song twice before going on to the next one.

Great-Aunt Frieda nodded and smiled through each song, sometimes tapping her foot in time with the music. Moishy noticed that she kept touching her ear. He remembered that she wore a hearing aid. I hope it's not giving her any trouble, he thought. She looks like she's enjoying the concert so much, it would be a shame to miss any. He sang louder.

After awhile Great-Aunt Frieda stopped fiddling with her ear and settled into her knitting. Once in awhile she would smile and nod at Moishy. Moishy sang and sang for her, every song that he could remember, as loudly as he could.

"My mother always helps me with my homework!" Mashie crossed her arms and pouted.

"But, Mashie," Yochie exclaimed. "You're not asking me to help you, you're asking me to do it for you. Stop it, Berel." Berel was kicking her under the table.

"That's how my mother helps me." Mashie's lower lip grew bigger.

"Mashie, you stick out that lip any further, and I'm going to trip on it," said Yochie. "Berel, cut it out!" Yochie made a swipe at his foot and missed.

Raizel stuck out her lower lip and giggled. "Trip on your lip," she said, and giggled again. Mashie glared at her.

"I'm glad someone's smiling," Yochie yelled as she grabbed for Berel's leg. This time she caught it and held on.

"Hey! Le'go!" Berel squirmed and tried to break free.

"Are you done kicking?" Yochie asked.

"Le'go my leg!" Berel pulled harder.

"When you tell me that you're done kicking I'll let go of your leg," said Yochie sweetly. She heard the refrigerator door open. "Kalman!" Dropping Berel's leg she ran across the kitchen just in time to grab the chopped liver out of Kalman's hands.

"But I'm hungry!" he protested.

"Okay, kid, but no chopped liver." She took him by the hand. "Let's go and eat your snack." Dragging him after her, Yochie went back to the table.

"Where are your aprons?" she asked. She was greeted with blank stares. "Your mother said that you have to eat with your aprons on," she tried again. "Where are they?"

"I'll get them," said Berel sullenly. He went to a drawer and started to pull everything out.

"Oh no, Berel, not again!" Yochie figured out which were the aprons and stuffed everything else back in the drawer.

After everyone was set up, Yochie uncovered the snack. Oh no, she thought. Harman's biscuits!

Every child in Bloomfield dreaded Harman's biscuits. They were the driest, dullest, most tasteless biscuits imaginable. Yochie said about them that she would rather eat cardboard, and here they were. Yochie forced a smile.

"Wow, what a great snack!" she exclaimed brightly. "Here you go!" She gave out the biscuits. The children just stared at them. Finally Berel made a *brachah* and took a small bite. With glum expressions, the other children also began to eat. Except Zalman.

"I thought you were hungry," Yochie said to him.

"Not that hungry," said Zalman.

"Zalman never eats a snack," Mashie informed him.

"Why not?" asked Yochie, thinking of the chopped liver.

"He doesn't like these biscuits." Mashie took another tiny bite of hers.

"But you don't have them every day, do you? For sure your mother only bought them because there was nothing else in the store, or something."

"We have them every day," said Mashie. "None of us likes them." She took another tiny bite.

These poor kids! thought Yochie. If I had to eat these biscuits every day, I'd go out of my mind.

"We never get sweets," said Raizel matter-of-factly.

"Never?"

"Never!" said Berel emphatically.

"Ima says we can have them by other people, but she won't buy them," said Mashie.

As they spoke, Zalman slipped off his chair and started towards the refrigerator. Yochie grabbed him.

While her back was turned, Berel took one of Raizel's biscuits. Raizel screamed.

"Berel! Raizel, why are you screaming? I thought you didn't like them anyway?" Yochie held Zalman with one hand while he transferred the biscuit from Berel's plate to Raizel's. Berel grabbed it and smashed it.

"You goniff," cried Mashie, and raised her hand to hit Berel. Raizel screamed louder.

"STOP!" Something about Yochie's tone made all the children turn to her. "Stop! Wait! I have an idea...a real fun idea." Yochie put on a secret smile. "This is the best idea ever, you'll see." The children watched her, fascinated. "You just sit in your places, and I'll show you my idea. Good. Sit down." The children sat down and watched Yochie, who backed away towards the sink.

An idea, an idea — please, Hashem, give me an idea! she thought as she tried to look as exciting as she could. I need an idea. She bumped into the sink. Help! she thought. She straightened up and put her hands in her pockets. "My idea...my idea....is..."

The children leaned forward. Yochie felt inside her pocket. A wonder ball? No. Rubber bands? No! What's that bag? Aha!

"My idea is...," Yochie whispered. "Candy!" Yochie whipped out a bag of gumdrops, malt balls, and assorted other sweeties. She'd put them there in case she'd need them, and then she'd totally forgotten about them.

The children sat mesmerized. They stared at the candy as if they'd never seen sweets before.

"Now, kiddies, we're going to play a little game...," said Yochie with a big smile. "And the prizes are right in the palm of my hand." Just like these kids, Yochie thought triumphantly.

Mrs. Freulich arrived at five-thirty. She opened the back door and called, tentatively, "Yochie? Children?" Tiptoeing in, she closed the door behind her. The kitchen was spotless, as she'd left it. There was no one there. "Yochie? Children?"

"We're upstairs, Mrs. Freulich," she heard Yochie call from the playroom. Mrs. Freulich hurried up the stairs.

"I'm so sorry, Yochie dear," she said as she burst into the playroom. "I got caught in traffic..." Her voice trailed off as she looked around the room. Everything was immaculate. The children were in pajamas, their faces shining. Yochie was sitting with a picture book on her lap; she'd been reading to them.

"Well," said Mrs. Freulich. "Well, I see you really are a manager. I always said your mother was a remarkable woman, and I can see how she's trained you..." She hesitated. "Did everything go smoothly?"

"No problem." Yochie smiled at the children. They grinned back.

Mrs. Freulich walked Yochie to the door, thanking her profusely every step of the way. When they got to the door, Mrs. Freulich asked with assumed casualness, "Do you think you could come back?"

"Sure," said Yochie. "Why not?"

"Wonderful, wonderful. Goodbye, Yochie darling!" Mrs. Freulich waved cheerfully.

"Goodbye, Mrs. Freulich!" Yochie skipped down the front steps and out the garden gate.

Walking down the street towards home, Yochie couldn't help humming a little tune. And in her pocket she crinkled an empty plastic bag.

The last note still hung in the air as Great-Aunt Frieda waved goodbye to Moishy. Smiling, she went inside to wash up her tea things. When she finished she returned to the living room to put away her knitting. In the hall she stopped and fingered her ear.

The telephone rang. She changed direction and went into the kitchen.

"Hello?"

"Hello?"

"Frieda, this is Faige. Were you home five minutes ago?"

"Hello, Faige. Yes, I was. As a matter of fact, I just saw my nephew off. Why do you ask?"

"Because I called, and you didn't answer."

Great-Aunt Frieda laughed. "I'm sorry, I didn't hear the phone. You see, I had my hearing aid turned off!"

7
Chezky's Diary #2

CLICK

Welcome once again to the diary of Yechezkel Baker!

What can I tell you? Things are really roaring here at the Bakers. The chesed project is in top gear, and we have chesed coming out of our ears.

Tikva is wowing them at the Center for the Blind, Dina has packed enough food for the entire Jewish population of Russia and lands east. Zahava and Yochie are "Babysitter's Best," and Rivka is single-handedly teaching a very thorough second grader. All out of the kindness of their hearts!

And how about the boys? Moishy Baker is keeping a lonely widow, Great-Aunt Frieda, well entertained. Donny is doing the same for Saraleh. And what about Chezky?...

I have been helping Mr. Schwartz and, boy, did he need help! We've spent a couple of days working in the garden. I worked hard, and even Charley helped. We worked so hard that Mr. Schwartz was speechless!

I figure that we're doing an extra-special job because, when I was out with Ima, I saw Mr. Schwartz going into a gardening shop. I ran after him and asked him what he was buying (if it was something heavy I would have offered to carry it.) Mr. Schwartz was real surprised to see me! When he got over his surprise he told me he was buying some seed. (He didn't need my help to carry it.) I figure that he wouldn't be buying seed unless we were really ahead in the gardening.

Doing chesed makes you feel so good! Everyone is in a good mood. Well, almost everyone. Bracha is still moping around the house. No one knows what's wrong with her, and she isn't telling. She didn't get into the chesed project. Too bad, maybe she'd be happier now if she did. Ima always says the surest road to happiness is helping other people.

The other person who is not so happy is Donny. He's okay during the day, and he really isn't so bad off at night...as long as he's in my bed! I haven't been sleeping very well, and neither has he when he has one of his nightmares. None of them has been as bad as the first one; he doesn't wake the whole house up any more...

But I sure don't sleep much (yawn)...

"CHEZKY! DINNER!"

See ya later, diary!

CLICK

8

"Can You Do Me a Favor?"

hezky, what took you so long?" Rivka demanded.

"We've been waiting for you, you know," said Yochie.

"We're starving!" Moishy exclaimed, clutching his stomach.

"I...uh...," Chezky stammered.

"He was with that tape recorder," Zahava announced. "It's your fault!" she added, pointing at Yochie.

Yochie sat up and looked all around her, as if she was searching for the person Zahava was pointing to. Then she looked back at Zahava. "Do you mean me? she squeaked, pointing to herself.

"Yes, you! You started him on that diary" Zahava tossed her head in the direction of the upstairs.

"I was just trying to improve his mind!" Yochie defended herself. "He was beginning to think like a baseball!"

"Hey!" Chezky protested.

"Enough!" said Mr. Baker. "Go wash!"

"What's for supper?" Chezky asked, as he let his father propel him towards the kitchen.

"Sloppy Joes..."

Chezky was gone.

The children scrambled into the kitchen without protesting. Everyone liked Sloppy Joes! "Boy, does something smell good!" said Moishy, sniffing the air as he waited his turn at the sink.

"I thought you helped with dinner," said Dini.

"I did. Although Ima and Rivka did most of the work," said Moishy, "I can appreciate my own handiwork, can't I?" He took up the cup and washed his hands. After saying the brachah, he tossed the towel to Dini and raced into the dining room.

"*BARUCH ATAH...*"

"I think the next-door neighbors can hear that," giggled Tikva to Yochie.

"*...HAMOTZI LECHEM MIN HA'ARETZ!*"

"The next-door neighbors," Yochie quipped. "How about the Chinese?" They giggled together.

"Get washing up there," Rivka said. "We don't have all night."

One by one the Bakers washed and sat down to eat. Soon, nothing could be heard but exclamations of pleasure.

"Ima, this is too good!" said Yochie.

"Wow, you put in mushrooms!" Chezky exclaimed.

"Pass the chili sauce, please," Moishy asked.

"*More* chili sauce?" Rivka replied.

"Yes, if you don't mind."

"It's your stomach."

"Donny, don't pick it up in your hands!" Everyone looked at Donny, who was holding his food by his fingers. There was tomato sauce all over his shirt and around his plate. Donny, about to take a bite, looked at his family and then at his dripping sandwich.

"Why not?" he asked.

"Because this is one sandwich that we eat with a knife and fork," Rivka exclaimed. "Oh, look at him!'

Mrs. Baker jumped up from her place and grabbed the roll of paper towels which, during the week, was always on the table. Deftly she extricated the sandwich from Donny's hands and began to clean him up.

Saraleh looked at him with wide eyes. "Donny, you're a mess."

Donny looked at his shirt as his mother wiped his hands. "I guess so," he said. He looked up. "Will someone cut my food?"

Mrs. Baker laughed, and the rest of the family joined in. "After I get you cleaned up, I'll cut it for you."

"Me too," said Saraleh, still looking at Donny. "I don't want to look like that!"

"I'll cut for you," Rivka told her. The rest of the family went back to eating — except Moishy, who was still looking at Donny.

"I guess that's what you'd call correct nomenclature," he said.

"Most people call it a Sloppy Joe," said Chezky, putting more chili sauce on his.

Mr. Baker laughed. "Correct nomenclature means that you're calling something by the right sort of name," he explained to Chezky. "Sloppy Joe is a very good descriptive name for this kind of sandwich."

"You're telling me," said Moishy. He took his eyes away from Donny and continued eating.

"Our names aren't very descriptive," said Yochie after a minute.

"Ima and Abba are," said Tikva.

"I meant first names." Yochie put a big bite in her mouth. "What does my name have to do with anything?" The words came out muffled.

"Yochie, we can't understand you," Dina intoned.

Yochie swallowed. "I said, 'What does my name have to do with anything?'"

"Tikva's name means a lot," said Zahava. "Tikva means hope." Tikva smiled.

"Saraleh certainly is a princess," said Rivka, rolling her eyes to the ceiling.

"That's right," Saraleh agreed.

"What about Moishy?" Yochie asked. "No one pulled him out of the water.

"But he's a genius," Chezky put in. "Like the original Moshe Rabbeinu." Moishy blushed.

"From your mouth to God's ears," muttered Mr. Baker.

"What about Zahava?" asked Yochie.

"Fits," said Moishy.

"I think that's a compliment," said Zahava. "Pass the salad."

They ate quietly for awhile. Then Yochie took up the discussion again.

"Doesn't Dina come from the word *din*, meaning justice?" she asked.

"Fits," said Moishy.

"I think that's a compliment, too," said Dini, looking at Moishy. Moishy was eating busily and didn't look up.

"Ima's name fits," said Tikva. "She's as precious and beautiful as a rose."

Mrs. Baker blushed and smiled lovingly. "Thank-you, Tikki."

"Bracha's name fits too," said Dini.

Bracha smiled slightly but didn't say anything. She went on eating. The conversation wandered on to the topic of the week, *chesed*. Everyone spoke, interrupting and finishing each other's sentences in their excitement.

Everyone except Bracha. She followed the conversation but kept completely to herself. Mrs. Baker watched her.

I wish she would tell us what is bothering her, she thought. I'm getting very worried.

Yochie gave a comic rendition of her babysitting experiences. The family roared with laughter, all except Bracha, who merely smiled politely. Mrs. Baker pressed her lips together and didn't say a thing.

Mr. Baker noticed his wife's expression and, with his eyes, asked her what was wrong. She looked towards Bracha. He looked at her too, and his face became more serious.

"So, Bracha...," he began,

"Abba, Abba, you have to hear this." Chezky tugged at his sleeve. Mr. Baker, distracted, turned towards him.

Mrs. Baker wasn't distracted, though, and neither was Bracha.

Well, it's her turn to wash up tonight, Mrs. Baker thought. I'll work along with her and see if I can get her to talk about it.

After the meal, when everyone had finished clearing, Bracha and Mrs. Baker were left alone in the kitchen. Bracha washed the dishes, and her mother dried.

"Thank you for keeping me company, Ima," Bracha said after a while.

"It's a pleasure," said Mrs. Baker. They worked quietly for five minutes. When Mrs. Baker saw that Bracha wasn't going to start a conversation, she decided to start one herself.

"How did that math test go?" she asked.

Bracha seemed to tense up — or was it just her mother's imagination? "Okay," she said guardedly.

"Did you get the test back yet?"

"Yes."

This is like pulling teeth, thought Mrs. Baker. "So, how did you do?"

"Okay." Bracha rinsed a plate slowly, swirling the water around and around.

"What grade did you get?" Mrs. Baker persisted.

"A hundred," said Bracha in a soft voice.

"Wonderful!" Mrs. Baker exclaimed.

"I guess," Bracha sighed.

Mrs. Baker stopped drying the plate she was holding and moved closer to her daughter. "Aren't you glad you got that mark?"

Bracha stopped rinsing the plate in her hand. She stood looking into the sink, letting the water run. "Ima..." She hesitated.

The kitchen door burst open, and Donny ran in with Saraleh right behind him. "Ima!" they cried. From down the hall they heard Yochie growling: "I'm coming to get you!"

Saraleh and Donny squealed and clung onto their mother. The kitchen door banged open again, and Yochie stomped in.

"Groowrrr!" she said. "Where are those little kids that have to go to bed?"

Donny and Saraleh laughed and squealed. "No!" yelled Saraleh. "We don't want to go to bed!"

"Yochie," Mrs. Baker laughed. "I'm not sure this is the most effective method to get them to bed."

"You'll see," Yochie growled. "Anyone not in bed gets...TICKLED!" She roared and lurched towards Donny and Saraleh. They screamed, dodged past her, and ran out of the kitchen. "See?" said Yochie. "No problem." She stuck her hands in her skirt pockets and strolled out of the kitchen. Mrs. Baker laughed again and took up another plate to wipe. "That Yochie! Did you know that Mrs. Freulich can't stop raving about her?"

"I'll bet." Bracha turned back to the sink.

"Now," said Mrs. Baker. "Where were we?"

Chezky came through the back door. "Hello," he said. "Still doing dishes?"

"Chezky, what happened to your pants?" Mrs. Baker looked at him, horrified. Bracha stared at him for a moment, then went back to her dishes.

Chezky looked down at his pants. From the knee down they were plastered with mud.

"Oh," he said.

"What happened?" asked Mrs. Baker. "And don't come any farther — your shoes are muddy too."

Chezky looked up. "I left my glove and ball at Mr. Schwartz's when I went to help him today," he explained. "I put them in the bushes where no one would see them. I forgot about them until after supper when I went back to get them. I guess Mr. Schwartz watered the bushes or something. Where there was dirt, there is now mud."

Mrs. Baker shook her head. "Take off your shoes here. And your socks. Hold up your pant legs and walk, carefully, to the bathroom. It's a good thing it's a bath night."

"With Chezky, every night is bath night," Bracha quipped.

Chezky stuck out his tongue in a friendly way. So did Bracha. Mrs. Baker watched as Chezky carried out her instructions.

"Well, that's that," she said after Chezky left. She saw the pile of dishes in the dish rack. "You've been busy," she commented, and took up a dish to dry.

"You know, Ima," Bracha said. "It's kind of interesting that the rest of the family is involved with *chesed* right now."

"Yes," said Mrs. Baker, encouraging her. "Why do you say that?"

"Well, you see..."

There was a small explosion from upstairs. Mrs. Baker and Bracha looked at each other with wild eyes and ran out of the kitchen.

They ran up the stairs and looked for the source of the bang. From Moishy's room, green smoke was wafting out the door! They could hear the sound of coughing. Mrs. Baker rushed to the door.

"What happened?" she asked wildly.

"It's alright, dear," said Mr. Baker. He was coughing and laughing. Moishy was also coughing and laughing. "Everything is under control."

"Are you kidding me?" Mrs. Baker looked at her husband as if he'd gone out of his mind. "What's all this?" She batted at the smoke.

"Just a little experiment." Mr. Baker stopped coughing and cleared his throat. "Go back to what you were doing. We'll take care of everything."

Mrs. Baker eyed him apprehensively. "That's what I'm afraid of," she said. Reluctantly, she turned and left.

At the top of the stairs Bracha turned to her mother and said, "I'll take care of the rest of the kitchen. You don't have to come down if you don't want to."

I can't believe how things can go wrong, Mrs. Baker thought. Just as Bracha was going to open up, we get all of these interruptions. She gave up. "Okay, Bracha," she said. "Thank you very much."

"Nothing to thank," said Bracha. "It's supposed to be my job." She ran down the stairs. Mrs. Baker went down the hall to make sure Donny and Saraleh were in bed.

"What a gorgeous day!" said Zahava. "I love this weather."

"Mmmmmm," Tikva agreed, smelling the breeze. "Not too hot and not too cold."

The quintuplets were walking to school. Today, as she did once in a while, Bracha joined them. She felt like the company of her own family.

The sky was a clear blue, dotted here and there by swiftly moving, fluffy clouds. The breeze blew a fresh scent into their faces — the smell of grass, fresh earth, and early flowers.

"I don't even know why I brought a sweater," said Yochie. She took off her sweater and tied it around her waist.

"Yochie, don't do that!" Zahava exclaimed.

"Why not?"

"It looks so awful!" She tugged at Yochie's book bag, which was on her back. "Take this off, and I'll fix you up." Yochie took off her backpack, and Zahava arranged her sweater across her shoulders.

"There," she said "Isn't that better?"

"I don't know. I can't see it."

"It is better," said Rivka after eyeing her critically. "Much better."

"And better for the sweater too," said Dini.

"How do I carry my book bag?" Yochie asked.

"In your hand," said Zahava. "That way you don't mess up the sweater, and you don't look like a pack horse."

Yochie hefted her book bag in one hand. "I may not look as much like a pack horse, but I feel more like one."

Zahava sniffed.

"Alright, alright, I'll try it!" Yochie trudged down the block.

Bracha laughed at this little interchange between her sisters. She wondered how long Yochie would last with the sweater on her shoulders.

The girls walked along, enjoying the sunshine. Zahava sighed.

"What was that for?" Rivka asked.

"I was just thinking about my afternoon with Ima," said Zahava.

"I still don't understand what was so great." Yochie squinted up at the sky. "You only went to Ho-Ho's."

"It wasn't the ice cream, although that was yummy." Zahava licked her lips at the memory. "It was having Ima to myself for two whole hours! We got to talk about all kinds of stuff that we never have time to talk about at home. That was really neat." Zahava smiled happily.

"That sounds good to me," said Dini.

"Me too," said Rivka. "Although Ima is available if something serious comes up, she doesn't often have time to just shmooze."

"I guess I see," said Yochie. "And ice cream isn't a bad thing to shmooze over." She rubbed her stomach. Suddenly, she sighted a friend. "Chani!" she shouted. "I have to tell Chani something," she said to the others. "CHANI!" Yochie slung her book bag over her shoulder and began to run.

"Yochie! Your sweater!" Dini called after her. She picked up the sweater from where it fell on the sidewalk and dusted it off.

Zahava watched her. "Oh well," she sighed. "It was nice while it lasted."

"I'll give it to her," Dini volunteered and trotted after Yochie.

Zahava stretched her face towards the sky. "It's too gorgeous a day to hurry," she said.

"Mmmmm," Bracha agreed. She walked a little slower and eventually fell behind the other girls.

All of this gorgeous weather doesn't solve my problem, she thought. That was interesting — what Zahava was saying, about having Ima all to herself. I didn't think that Ima could help me. I wasn't even going to ask her until last night when we were doing the dishes. Then when I was going to talk to her we had all of those interruptions!

She hurried up and caught up to her sisters.

"Rivka," she panted. "Who has the next date with Ima?"

"I don't know," Rivka replied, a little surprised. "I don't think it's been decided yet."

"Would you mind if I went next?" Bracha asked.

"No," said Rivka slowly. "I guess not."

"I wouldn't mind," said Tikva.

"I've already had mine," said Zahava. "I have to wait a long time for the next one."

"Thanks. I'll ask the others later." Bracha smiled in satisfaction.

As they approached the building, Rivka glanced at her watch. "Help!" she said. "We walked too slowly! It's one minute until the bell!" She broke into a run, the other girls running after her.

"Hurry!" they heard a voice yell. There was Yochie at their classroom window! They sped up, except for Bracha. She was trying to get into the classroom just as the bell rang.

If I get there at exactly the right time, no one will be able to talk to me. She slowed down even more. Children streamed past her, including girls from her own class.

"Hi, Bracha!" said one as she ran past. Bracha nodded to her. She kneeled down as if she was tying her shoe. *When is that bell going to ring? Rivka's watch must have been fast.*

The halls began to empty out. Bracha walked slower still. *Any slower and I will be walking backwards,* she joked to herself, but the joke did little to lift the dread from her heart.

BRRINNGG!!! The bell rang just above her head. Bracha jumped up and rushed for the door. She didn't want to be late either. She slipped into her seat.

Made it! she thought. She dug into her book bag and took out her siddur. Looking around she noticed that her teacher still hadn't arrived. The girls around her were talking.

"Hey, Bracha?" said a familiar voice.

Bracha froze. Looking up, she said without enthusiasm: "Oh hi, Naomi."

"Hi there," Naomi said brightly. Bracha's heart sank as she heard the familiar words, "Hey, Bracha, can you do me a little favor?"

9
More Favors

You don't know how frustrating it's been," said Zahava as she reached into the closet and took out a skirt.

Rivka sat on the bed with her guitar. "I'll bet it's been very frustrating," she said sympathetically. She strummed and sang: "Frustration! Frus-ster-ra-shon!"

Zahava laid the skirt out on her bed and went to the dresser. "That's right!" she smiled at Rivka. "First I had that job with the Cohens, but she only needed me once; when her regular babysitter couldn't make it. Then I thought I was going to work for Mrs. Levin, but that didn't work out either." Zahava took a brightly colored sweatshirt and tights from her drawer and went back to her bed. "I looked and looked, but it seemed that every single *chesed* job in town was taken."

"*Oy! Oy! Oy!*" Rivka strummed and sang.

"There were all of you, and the boys, doing *chesed* like mad — and there was I, doing nothing!" Rivka played a sour chord and made a face.

"Exactly!" Zahava nodded. "Then Mrs. Cohen called back and said that her regular babysitter had quit, and did I want a job!" Rivka strummed triumphantly as Zahava spoke. "So now I have a regular job, with a family I know. Those kids are so good and cute too!" Rivka plucked out "Mary Had a Little Lamb" on the guitar.

"I'm going to take them to the park today," Zahava continued. "That's why I picked out my dark corduroy skirt; it won't matter how dirty I get. I want them to have fun."

Rivka played *"Ashreinu"* and smiled and nodded.

"Do you think this will look alright together?" Zahava asked, pointing to the clothes laid out on the bed.

Rivka stopped playing her guitar and looked. "Zahava," she said, "if anyone could make an old corduroy skirt look good, you can." She started playing *"Sheker hachein..."*

"Okay, okay, I get the hint." Zahava laughed and began to change her clothing.

Rivka stopped playing and examined the sheet music in front of her. She had recently started guitar lessons again, being dissatisfied with her playing. Her parents had found an excellent guitar teacher, and Rivka was loving it. It was hard, though. Rivka examined the new piece her teacher gave her with some trepidation. She read through the music, fingering some of the more difficult chords.

"What's everyone else doing today?"

"Huh?" Rivka looked up. Zahava had already dressed and was brushing her hair.

"What is everyone else doing today?" Zahava repeated herself.

"Oh." Rivka rested her guitar on her knees. "Dini has another food-packing session, but everyone else seems to have the day off. Not me, though. When I finish here I have to go and tutor."

"Same little girl?" Zahava asked.

"Yup. I finally got her to stop reading all that stuff at the beginning of the book. She's coming along nicely. She's really determined." Rivka picked up her guitar again and put her fingers on the strings. "I wish I was like that."

Zahava finished with her hair and went to the door. "So most of the Bakers are having a quiet afternoon at home."

"Most of them," Rivka agreed absently. "Oh, Yochie and Tikki are babysitting for the little kids. Bracha is going out for her day with Ima."

Bracha tapped on her mother's bedroom door. "I'm ready, Ima," she called softly.

"So am I," said Mrs. Baker, opening the bedroom door. Mrs. Baker was wearing a simple, navy blue knit suit. She had her *sheitel* on and a gold brooch pinned to her left shoulder.

"You look nice, Ima," Bracha told her.

"Thank you," Mrs. Baker smiled. "You look nice too!" Bracha was glad that she'd been extra careful how she dressed. After all, you don't go out with your mother every day — and she wanted her mother to be proud of her.

"I just have to warn the troops," said Mrs. Baker, with a wry grin.

"Right." Bracha grinned back.

Yochie and Tikva were in the homework room: Tikva sitting at the computer, Yochie at the long table.

"We're on our way," said Mrs. Baker.

"Good," said Tikva. "Have a good time."

"Eat an ice cream for me!" said Yochie wistfully.

"There's ice cream in the freezer," Mrs. Baker told her. "You can eat one yourself."

"It's not the same as Ho-Ho's," said Yochie. "But don't vorry about me," she said in a fake Yiddish accent. "I'll be alright."

"Yochie!"

The boys were in Moishy's room, playing Risk.

"Now for Brazil!" said Moishy, rubbing his hands together. He snickered.

"You haven't won yet," said Chezky shaking his dice in his hand. "We'll see what will be!"

"Boys, we're leaving," said Mrs. Baker.

"By the time you come back, Mother," said Moishy dramatically, "I shall be emperor of the world."

"Good luck, your majesty."

"We'll see, we'll see," said Chezky ominously.

Donny and Saraleh were in Saraleh's room, playing house. Donny, with the help of many pillows, had constructed a car on the bed, and as far as they could tell was driving to work.

"I can't believe this traffic!" he said.

Mrs. Baker laughed. "You sound just like your father!" Donny took a small book from his pocket and sat over it, reading and crooning to himself. "What happened to your drive?" his mother asked him.

"Lots of traffic!" said Donny without looking up from his book.

"So what are you doing?"

"I know!" said Bracha, her eyes twinkling. "Whenever Abba is stuck in traffic and it looks like he'll have to wait awhile, he always takes out a *sefer!*" She burst out laughing. Mrs. Baker joined her.

"Okay, Donny," she said. "We just want to tell you that we're leaving. Yochie and Tikva are in charge. Abba's in the cottage, working."

Donny looked up. "Don't worry," he said. "I'm watching Saraleh."

Mrs. Baker smiled. "Thank you, Donny. Now we just have to tell your father, and we're off." She led the way downstairs.

"By the time we tell everyone were leaving, it'll almost be time to come home," Bracha complained.

"I know," Mrs. Baker agreed. "But it's the *menschlich* thing to do."

Before they could go out to Mr. Baker's law office/cottage, the back door opened and he came into the kitchen, Rachel Ahuva in his arms.

"Shoshana, I'm glad I met you," he said briskly. "What's up?"

"I have an emergency meeting with Mr. Wein."

"That's a little problem," said Mrs. Baker. "You were going to watch Rachel Ahuva." She turned around to go back upstairs. "I'll go up and tell the girls they have to watch her."

"No, wait," said Mr. Baker. "Mr. Wein got a big kick out of the baby last time he was here. I thought I'd take her along."

Mrs. Baker looked doubtful. "If you're sure it will be alright..."

"I think it will. She'll soften the old guy up, won't you, sweetie?" he said bouncing the baby in his arms.

"Up, up!" Rachel Ahuva replied.

"Well then, that's that," said Mrs. Baker. "Just tell the girls you're going, please. We shouldn't be home too late."

"Fine."

As she got into the car. Bracha felt a few butterflies in her stomach. I hope we get to talk about my problem, she thought. I hope Ima can find a solution.

Afternoon settled over the old Wharton mansion. Outside there were one or two birds singing. From down the block dogs barked and children played. In the homework room the windows were open, letting in the fresh, spring air. Tikva typed on the computer. Yochie leaned back with her feet on the table, dreaming. Tikva spoke without looking up.

"Yochie, get your feet off the table — we put *sifrei kodesh* there."

"How did you know that my feet were on the table?" said Yochie, sitting up.

"I can tell when you lean your chair back by the way it squeaks," Tikva told her. "From there it was just simple deduction."

"I was just thinking — " Yochie began. Down the hall the telephone rang. "Somebody get the phone!" she hollered.

"Why don't you get it yourself?" Tikva asked.

"Those boys aren't doing anything," she answered. "And besides, they're closer." The phone rang again.

"The pho-one!" shouted Yochie louder.

"I don't think they can hear you." Another ring.

Yochie rushed to the door of the homework room. "The PHONE!" she hollered.

"Just go and get it yourself," Tikva chuckled. The phone rang again.

"GET THE PHONE!"

"Yochie!" Yochie ran down the hall. *R-r-r-ring*!

The door of Moishy's room flew open, and Moishy jumped out, crashing right into her.

"*Ow!* Never mind," said Yochie through gritted teeth. "I'm getting it myself."

"Sorry," said Moishy rubbing his arm where he had collided with Yochie. The telephone rang again. Yochie dashed into the study and grabbed the receiver.

"Hello? Baker residence," she panted.

"Hello, may I speak with Yochie?"

"Speaking."

"Yochie! This is Mrs. Freulich. When no one answered I was sure you were out, and I wouldn't have known what to do! I'm so glad you're home! Can you babysit for me right now? Something's come up and I have to go out. It will only be for an hour and a half..."

"I don't see why not, Mrs. Freulich," Yochie replied. "Especially since it's an emergency."

"Thank you so much!" said Mrs. Freulich. "How soon can you come?"

Yochie glanced at her watch and then at the study clock to make sure her watch was right. "In about fifteen or twenty minutes. Is that okay?"

"Perfect! Thank you again, darling. You're saving my life!" Mrs. Freulich hung up the phone.

Yochie trotted back down the hall to the homework room.

"Who was on the phone?" Tikva asked her.

"Mrs. Freulich. I have to babysit for her. It's an emergency."

"See?" said Tikva happily. "*Mitzvah gorreres mitzvah.*"

"Mmmm," said Yochie as she tied her shoes.

"I wish I was going to do my *chesed*," Tikva sighed.

"Can't you go?" Yochie asked her. "I thought this was a volunteer job. I didn't know that volunteer jobs had limited hours."

"Some do," said Tikva. "Actually, Miss Katz said that I could come any afternoon I want."

"So why don't you go?" said Yochie. "We can walk together, and I'll pick you up on my way back."

"What about Donny and Saraleh?" said Tikva doubtfully.

"The boys can watch them; it won't be for long."
Yochie ran a quick comb through her ponytail.

"Let's go ask them." They went down the hall to
Moishy's room.

"And now for Brazil," Chezky was saying as they
came in.

Moishy clutched his head in his hands and rocked
from side to side. "No, no, not Brazil," he cried.

"You took it from me," said Chezky as he shook his
dice. "Now I take it from you."

"If I can interrupt this great battle," said Yochie,
"Tikki and I are going out. Can you guys do us a favor
and watch Donny and Saraleh? We have to go and do
chesed."

"Sure, sure," said Moishy distractedly. "Please
don't take Brazil!"

"What?" Yochie looked at him as if he was crazy.

"He's talking to me," said Chezky.

"Oh." Yochie and Tikva left the room.

"And a one, and a two," said Chezky, shaking the
dice gleefully. Moishy leaned his head on one hand
and let his dice fall out of his hand. Then he shut his
eyes.

"Three sixes!" said an astonished Chezky.

"It figures..."

"No, you got three sixes!"

Moishy picked up his head and laughed. "Now
we'll see who gets Brazil!"

The Battle for South America went on for quite
awhile. At first it seemed that it would belong to
Moishy, then Chezky, then Moishy again.

"Whew!" said Moishy at last. "Don't you get the feeling that this isn't going anywhere?"

"Yeah," said Chezky glumly. He had just lost Argentina.

"What do you say we divide the world in half and call it quits?" Moishy suggested.

"Good idea." Chezky reached across the board and shook Moishy's hand.

"Moishy and Chezky Baker: Grand Dictators!"

"That's us!"

"Let's go get a snack!"

"Right!" The boys put all the game pieces in the box and deposited it in the hall closet on their way to the kitchen.

"You know," Moishy said some time later as he brushed crumbs from his lap, "I've got to think of a new way to entertain Great-Aunt Frieda."

"Yeah?"

"Yeah. I've sung her everything I know dozens of times." Moishy put his head in his hands and thought.

"What about reading to her?" Chezky put his hand in the cookie box that was on the table and felt around.

Moishy gave him a scathing look. "Really, Chezky!" he said.

"Well, it was an idea," said Chezky. He put his hand in the box up to his elbow. "How about playing with her?"

"What?'

Chezky took his hand out of the box and held it upside down. A small shower of crumbs fell onto the table. "You could play a game with her, like Risk."

"Risk? With Great-Aunt Frieda?"

"Why not?" Putting the box down with a sigh, Chezky licked his finger and picked up some of the crumbs. "Or chess, or something."

Moishy didn't reply. Chezky looked up from his crumb-picking, expecting Moishy to tell him he was crazy. Instead, Moishy was smiling from ear to ear.

"What a great idea!" he said. "Chezky, you're a genius."

"I am?" said Chezky, surprised. People rarely accused him of genius.

Moishy jumped up and took his cup to the sink. "I'll bet Great-Aunt Frieda would love to play chess with me."

"What if she doesn't know how to play?" Chezky licked a few more crumbs, then began to sweep the rest into a little pile.

"I'll teach her; that's no problem," said Moishy.

"Just like you taught other people. And then you slaughter them," Chezky swept the pile of crumbs onto his hand and poured them into his mouth.

"What are you talking about?"

"I mean, you teach them how to play but you never teach them how to win." Chezky dusted his hands on his pants.

"That's not true!" Moishy put his hands deep into his pockets. "But maybe I should let her win. Maybe it's not nice to beat a widow."

"I don't know if that's very honest," said Chezky thoughtfully.

"I guess you're right," said Moishy. "Anyway, I'm going to get the chessboard." He moved towards the door.

Chezky jumped up. "But what about the little kids? Someone's got to watch them."

"What's wrong with you?"

"If you're going to your *chesed*, then I want to go and do mine." Chezky stuck out his lower lip.

Moishy thought for a minute. "You're right," he said. "Those girls went off to *chesed*, dumping everything on us! Look," he said, pointing up to the clock. "Everyone's going to be home any minute. We can go and leave Donny in charge."

"You're right!" They ran up to Saraleh's room.

"Donny!" Moishy shouted as they ran through the door.

Donny jumped. He was still in his make-believe car. "What?" he said.

"Donny, Chezky and I have to go out. Can you watch Saraleh for a little while? Someone's for sure going to be home very soon," Moishy said.

"I *am* watching Saraleh," Donny told him.

"Good. Then you can keep doing it," Moishy turned to leave.

"Of course I'll keep doing it!"

"I'll be at Great-Aunt Frieda's." Moishy called over his shoulder.

"And I'll be at Mr. Schwartz's!" Chezky added.

"Okay, okay," said Donny in a tired, grown-up voice.

"Bye!" called Saraleh.

Donny got out of his car and closed the pillow-door. Coming over to Saraleh he bellowed, "I'm home!"

"Hello, dear," said Saraleh. "Sit down and I'll give you something to eat."

Donny sat at the small play table and waited. Saraleh soon came with some toy dishes on a tray. "Here," she said.

Donny stared at what she brought. Each dish held shapeless red, yellow, and blue blobs.

"What is it?" he asked.

"Supper."

"No. I mean what's for supper?"

"Meat loaf, potatoes, and salad. And cookies," said Saraleh.

Donny looked at the plates again. "I mean, what's it made out of?"

"Play-Doh," Saraleh told him. "Eat; it's good." She smiled.

Donny took up his fork and knife and pretended to eat, but somehow his heart wasn't in it. "I thought you weren't allowed to play with Play-Doh in your room," he said after awhile.

"I'm not getting any on the rug," Saraleh said calmly. She was dressing one of the dolls. "I'm going out."

"To where?"

"I'm taking the baby on a picnic." She tried one hat on the doll, then changed it for another.

"Oh."

Saraleh took up a small basket she'd filled with more "food." "Goodbye, dear," she said. "I'll be back soon." She walked out of the room.

Donny waited for awhile. Then he said out loud: "I think I'll walk over to my office." He went down the hall to his room.

When he walked into his room he felt as if he'd walked out of the game. He stood for a minute in the middle of the room, wondering what to do. After a mighty yawn, he flung himself down on his bed. Eventually, he closed his eyes.

After a moment he opened them a crack, just enough to let in some light. Then he closed them, tight, opened them, then closed them again. And opened them, sighing.

Without wanting to, he began to think about the closet. Since that day he hadn't set foot in the blue guest room. He knew the closet was still there, its door chipped from Abba's screwdriver. Sometimes he felt like it was waiting for him to come back. Sometimes he felt like it could come after him, that it wanted to swallow him up.

"I'm not scared," he whispered. "I wasn't scared." He could feel a lump forming in his throat, and tears came to his eyes.

"Stupid," he said, as he wiped his eyes on his sleeves. "Stupid crying. I don't want to be scared."

He looked over to Chezky's bed. Then he walked across the room and got into it, pulling up the covers. It felt empty without Chezky.

He didn't want to go into Chezky's bed at night. He always started off in his own bed, brave as could be. But then, he'd start to feel the closet coming, with the dark and the monsters. And suddenly his own bed would seem a very scary place to be.

I don't want to be a scaredy-cat, he thought sadly. Chezky knows that I am a scaredy-cat. I wonder if he told anyone? Ima hasn't said anything.

I don't want to be a scaredy-cat. I'll bet everyone knows that I am one. Donny sniffed and buried his head in Chezky's pillow.

10
Where Is Saraleh?

Mrs. Baker drove carefully into the parking
lot next to Ho-Ho's.

"I hope we'll find a parking spot," she
said peering over the steering wheel.

"Me too!" agreed Bracha fervently.

They drove towards the back of the parking lot.
"It's very crowded," Mrs. Baker remarked.

"It always is." Bracha looked out of the window,
scanning her side of the parking lot. "Look," she exclaimed suddenly. "Someone's going out!" Several
yards ahead, a blue compact was pulling out of a
parking space.

"Do you think we'll get our big monster in that
space?"

"Why not?" Bracha asked. "Aren't all spaces the
same?"

"In theory," said Mrs. Baker as she watched the compact pull out. She put the van into gear when the car drove away.

On either side of the parking space, there were two large cars, crowding the space in between.

"Will we get in?" That space looked small!

"With your help, we will!" Mrs. Baker looked very determined. "Hop out and direct me!"

Bracha jumped out of the van and stood at the front of the spot. Mrs. Baker backed up a little and began to ease in.

"To the left," said Bracha, indicating with her hands. "To the left a little more...a little more... Right! Good, good." Bracha beckoned with both hands. "Great! Stop!" Mrs. Baker braked and turned off the motor.

"Yay!" Bracha applauded. Mrs. Baker clasped both hands and held them over her head.

"That was one tight space, Ima," said Bracha. "And you did it!" Bracha examined the space between their van and the car next to it. "Are you going to be able to get out of there?"

Mrs. Baker opened the car door a crack. "I think so; I don't want to knock into the car next to us." She eased herself through the half-open door. "Made it!" After locking the door she slung her handbag over her shoulder.

Up on the sidewalk Mrs. Baker gave Bracha's shoulder a squeeze. "You gave great directions," she said. "I couldn't have done it without you."

Bracha felt warm all over, and very close to her mother. She hurried ahead a few steps and held the door of the restaurant open.

"Thank you!" said Mrs. Baker.

"You're welcome."

Ho-Ho's was crowded. At the counter stood mothers with children, teenagers, and one father who looked out of place.

"What will it be, Bracha?"

"I don't know..." Bracha went closer to the counter.

"Not that way," said Mrs. Baker. "We're going to sit in a booth."

"In a booth? Goody!"

They sat down and made themselves comfortable. Mrs. Baker picked up her menu. This is no time to worry about calories, she thought.

Bracha bent down and studied her menu. Her eyes widened.

"I think I'll have a sundae with strawberry sauce," said Mrs. Baker.

How can Ima decide so fast? Bracha thought frantically. I don't want to make her wait. What should I get? A sundae? A triple shake? A...a...banana split?

"Can I have a banana split?"

Mrs. Baker smiled generously. "Whatever you want!"

"Then I'll have one," said Bracha positively. This is fun, she thought.

They ordered, Bracha hardly believing that she was going to get a banana split. Once she'd ordered one with a few friends, but she'd never had one all to herself.

"I hope I can finish it," she said without thinking.

"Don't worry about it," said Mrs. Baker. "If you don't finish it, I'll bring the leftovers to the kids."

"It will be melted!'

"They won't care."

Bracha giggled. She looked around the booth. It felt very private, with its high sides. Bracha liked the feeling of being private in public.

"So, Bracha, what's new?" Mrs. Baker looked at her oldest daughter with a warm smile.

"Well...the new book in my favorite series came out," Bracha gave her mother a sidelong glance. "You know, the one by Sefer Press. Miri Kramer read it and says it's great."

"I hope you'll be able to get your hands on it," said Mrs. Baker blandly.

"Me too," said Bracha, still looking at her mother.

Mrs. Baker laughed. "Okay, Bracha, I'll see what I can do. No promises." She looked away. "Oh look! Here comes our ice cream."

The banana split was beautiful. It had three scoops of ice cream: chocolate, vanilla, and strawberry with a banana underneath. It was smothered with fudge sauce and nuts, and topped with not one, but three, cherries. Bracha made her *brachos* and dug in.

"This is great!" she told her mother.

"Mmmm," said Mrs. Baker, her mouth full of ice cream.

They ate a while in silence. Finally, Mrs. Baker asked, "So how's school?"

Bracha's face fell. It was as if a cloud had come over the sun. Mrs. Baker looked at her sympathetically.

Bracha tried to be light. "Oh, you know, school is school. It has its ups and downs," she said.

"Yes?" asked Mrs. Baker. "Such as?"

Bracha shrugged.

"How's the schoolwork?"

Bracha looked more miserable. Could she be having trouble with her work? Mrs. Baker wondered. That wouldn't be very like Bracha.

"It's okay... I don't enjoy it as much as I used to," Bracha said in a low voice.

Mrs. Baker waited for her to continue.

"Ima, what do you think of copying?"

Mrs. Baker thought for a minute. What was Bracha trying to tell her? "Copying is a problem. It's sad when someone copies schoolwork. They don't learn at all, and they become very dependent on the person or persons they copy from. A person in that kind of situation can't be feeling very good about themselves..."

Mrs. Baker could see Bracha struggling with herself. She toyed with her half-finished banana split, smoothing down the sides of the different flavored ice creams.

"Ima, someone is copying from me," she said at last. She looked as if she wanted to cry.

"It seems that being copied from makes you very upset," said Mrs. Baker in a gentle voice.

"Oh, Ima, it does! There's this girl, she asks me for my homework every morning. I give it to her and I hate it! First of all, it's dishonest. She's not doing the homework, and she's getting credit. Not only that, but it makes me mad because I work so hard on my homework every night..."

"I know," said Mrs. Baker.

"...and she just copies it. She doesn't sit for hours — she's probably out having fun or something." Bracha took a deep breath and went on. "She's not a very good student; she always just gets by. When I first gave her homework, I wanted to do her a favor, help her out a little. I thought if she saw how to do it she would start doing it for herself. Now, I resent the whole thing and I feel bad. I'm trying to do a *chesed* but it's making me so angry..." Bracha toyed with her ice cream some more.

Thoughtfully, Mrs. Baker finished off the last bite of her sundae. Bracha looked at her, miserable and expecting the worst. "I think," said Mrs. Baker, "that maybe the first thing we have to do is to define what is a *chesed*..."

Donny sat up with a sigh. He went to the bathroom to look in the mirror. I don't want anyone to think I've been crying, he thought. After he washed his face he looked carefully at his reflection. Then he stuck his tongue out. His reflection stuck out its tongue out too.

With another sigh he went down to the kitchen to get a snack.

He found the empty cookie box on the kitchen table and turned it upside down.

"All gone," he said. "Today is not my day." Sticking his head into the pantry, he wondered if he was allowed to open another box. Not sure, he went to the refrigerator instead and took out an apple.

He dragged a chair over to the sink and washed the apple, then dried it, made a *brachah*, and bit into it.

"This is a good apple," he said out loud. He went to the screen door and looked out.

When I finish this apple I'll play with Saraleh again. I'm her babysitter, and I ought to be with her. She can watch herself while I eat my snack, and then I'll go to her.

Wow! Look at those clouds coming. Maybe it's gong to rain. Maybe there will be thunder. And lightning. From far away he saw Rivka, walking briskly. Before he'd finished half his apple, she was home.

"Hi, kiddo." She rubbed him on the head. He pulled away. "I'm glad I came home now; it looks like rain." She walked past him into the kitchen.

Donny turned back to the back door. The wind picked up and blew through the screen. The air smelled damp. Donny could hear a distant rumble of thunder.

"Boy, oh boy," said Rivka, coming up behind him. "I hope whoever is out there has a raincoat and umbrella. Where is everyone?"

"Yochie and Tikki went to do *chesed*. So did Moishy and Chezky," Donny told her.

"And they left you and Saraleh alone?" Rivka looked troubled.

"I'm babysitting," said Donny.

"What time did they leave?"

Donny shrugged. Before Rivka could speak, Donny pointed.

"Look," he said. "Here comes Zahava."

Rivka looked out the back door. It started to rain, a few drops, slowly. They splattered on the ground, making wet circles about the size of a dime.

"Look at her run," said Rivka.

Zahava sprinted across the garden and took the back steps in one bound. Rivka pulled open the back door, and Zahava catapulted into the kitchen.

"Just in time," she panted. "Just in time! *Baruch Hashem*, I got those kids home on time."

"*Baruch Hashem*, you got yourself home on time!"

"You said it! Boy, look at it come down!" The three children crowded around the back door and looked out at the rain. Big, gray clouds poured out rain onto the earth below. Puddles were forming and the gutters streamed.

"Whoever is out there now will be getting a shower with their clothes on," said Zahava.

"Really!" Rivka agreed. Donny giggled.

"Let's make some hot chocolate," said Rivka.

"Okay," Zahava agreed. "But we'd better make enough for everyone." The girls went to make hot chocolate. Donny stayed at the door.

Moishy and Chezky arrived together a moment later. Both of them were sopping wet.

"Is it raining?" Zahava asked, her face serious but her eyes twinkling mischievously.

"No, we took a shower with our clothes on," Moishy quipped.

Donny giggled. "See, what did I tell you?" Zahava told Rivka.

"What did you tell her?" Chezky asked.

"That anyone out in this rain will be getting a shower with their clothes on!" Zahava said triumphantly.

Moishy groaned. Chezky made a face.

"Go up and change," Rivka suggested. "We're making hot chocolate." The boys went upstairs. When they came down, the hot chocolate was on the table.

"Weren't you a little worried about leaving Donny alone with Saraleh?" Rivka asked Moishy as they drank.

"Nah!" said Moishy. "He did fine, didn't you, Donny?"

"Of course!" said Donny roundly.

"I don't know..." Rivka sipped at the hot chocolate.

"Where did you go?" Zahava asked Chezky.

"I went to help Mr. Schwartz," he answered. "He was very busy, so he asked me to take out Charley. We got caught in the rain! When we got back Charley messed up the whole kitchen. He shook himself so the water sprayed everywhere!" Chezky chuckled. "I was going to help Mr. Schwartz in the house because he was so busy, but suddenly he remembered that Charley had to go to the veterinarian. It's funny how many times Charley's had to go to the doctor lately...," he mused.

He turned to Moishy. "How did it go at Great-Aunt Frieda's? Did you teach her to play chess?"

"You were going to teach Great-Aunt Frieda how to play chess?" Rivka exclaimed.

"Yes," said Moishy shortly.

"And did you?"

"Yes."

"Oh wow, that must have been great; I wish I was there." Rivka grinned in excitement. "Tell us about it."

"Do you really want to know?"

"Yes!'

"Well, I took out the board and showed her the moves. She listened carefully and asked a couple of questions. Then she asked: 'If I understand correctly, the whole idea is to take the king?' So I said yes and we started to play." Moishy stopped speaking.

"What happened next?" Rivka urged him.

"I hope you gave her a chance," said Chezky.

"Give her a chance? Give her a chance?" Moishy exclaimed. "It was mate in three moves!" He put his head in his hands.

"You mean she beat you?" Chezky asked incredulously.

"In three moves," Moishy groaned. "Then she packed up the chessboard and said that she'd really enjoyed the game, but she was pretty busy and would call me if she needs any more visiting."

Chezky whistled. "I wish I'd been there!" said Rivka. "A new champion is crowned!"

Moishy groaned again.

Donny looked at Moishy in amazement. No one beat Moishy at chess. Everyone said so! His respect for Great-Aunt Frieda rose.

Everyone was talking at once. Chezky caught Donny's eye and winked at him. Donny remembered his job and decided to leave in search of Saraleh. No one noticed him going.

He went upstairs to his little sister's room and said, "Hello! I'm home!"

No one answered. Saraleh wasn't there. "Now where did she go?" he said, putting his small hands on his hips. "I'd better go and look for her."

"So we can conclude from this that a *chesed* isn't really a *chesed* unless it actually helps the person," said Mrs. Baker some time later. "Does that make sense?"

"Yes," said Bracha.

"So how does that fit into your situation?"

"Well," said Bracha, thinking hard, "when I started giving her the homework I thought I was doing a real favor. Maybe I was, once or twice. But as time went on she came to...depend on me. She stopped trying altogether."

"Go on."

"Now she's really in a mess. She's not improving, and maybe she's even getting worse because she's not studying at all. So I'm helping her get away with a lie,

and I'm helping her fall farther and farther behind."
Bracha sighed. "It wasn't really a *chesed*."

"And therefore you don't have to feel bad that you're feeling bad about it, right?"

"Right," Bracha sat back with a smile. She started eating her ice cream again, then stopped. "But Ima, what am I going to do?"

Mrs. Baker grimaced. "We still have a problem, don't we?"

"Yes!" Bracha wailed.

"Well, let's put on our thinking caps again."

Donny looked in all of the bedrooms. He looked in the study and the homework room. He looked in the living room and the dining room and, screwing up all of his courage, he even glanced quickly into the blue guest room.

"Boy, am I glad she wasn't in there," he said as he padded down the hall to the kitchen.

The same people were in the kitchen, involved in an animated conversation. Donny stood by the door, trying to decide what to do.

"Where's Donny?" asked Rivka.

"Here he is, by the door," Zahava told her.

"Good. We don't want to lose him again, do we Donny?" Donny shook his head. "And where is Saraleh?"

"Don't worry about Saraleh," Zahava told her. "Donny's taking care of her. Listen to this..."

Donny watched them talk for a minute, then he walked up to Moishy and tugged at his sleeve.

"I can't find Saraleh," he whispered.

"What?" said Moishy in a loud voice. "I can't hear you when you talk so softly. Quiet," he told the other children. "I can't hear Donny."

Everyone stopped talking and looked at Donny. "What is it Donny?" Moishy asked.

"It's Saraleh," Donny said miserably. "I don't know where she is."

"Isn't she in her room?" Chezky asked.

Donny shook his head. "No, I looked. I looked and looked, and I can't find her anywhere. I don't think she's in the house."

11
Panic!

Wow, Ima, it's raining!" Bracha looked out of the window next to the restaurant booth. "And hard!"

Mrs. Baker looked up. Outside, gray clouds were scuttling overhead, low in the sky. The parking lot was shiny black and wet, and rainwater ran down cars and dripped into iridescent puddles. "We were talking so much we didn't even notice the weather change."

"Can you believe it?" Bracha scraped her spoon along the bottom of her dish, scooping up the last of the ice cream. "Can you also believe that I finished this banana split?"

"Never underestimate a Baker!" Mrs. Baker intoned. Bracha giggled. "Let's go over our plan one more time, just to make sure that we've got it clear, okay?"

"Yes."

"You're going to, one, stop sharing your homework with this girl, since we've come to the understanding that it's not really a *chesed* and, two, approach the teacher and hint that she might need some extra attention. Right?"

"Right," said Bracha. "I guess. It's not going to be easy to tell this girl no; she might get very upset with me."

"That is a possibility." Mrs. Baker nodded.

"I don't want to hurt her feelings," Bracha added.

"I don't blame you," said Mrs. Baker understandingly. "Can you think of a way to say it that won't be so hurtful?"

Bracha sat and thought. "I guess there's no way that I'm not going to hurt her feelings at all..." She thought some more. "And I certainly don't want to lie!...I guess I just have to say it as it is: that I don't feel right about giving her the homework, that once or twice wasn't so bad but in giving her the homework every day I don't feel like I'm doing her a favor."

"Perhaps you could offer to help her?"

"Maybe, " said Bracha reluctantly. "It sounds like the right thing to do, but I can't say I really want to..."

Mrs. Baker let that pass. "Do you think you could say anything to boost her confidence in herself and help to convince her that you don't think she's a *nebech*?"

"I didn't think of that," said Bracha. "Maybe I could tell her that she really doesn't need that homework, that I was sure she could do fine without it... That sounds funny." Bracha made a face.

"Well, you're on the right track." Mrs. Baker shifted in her seat. "Look, it's clearing up." In the parking lot, the sun shone through a crack in the clouds, and the asphalt glittered. "What do you say we make tracks for home?"

"Good idea." Bracha and her mother said an after-*brachah* and went to pay. As they went out of Ho-Ho's, Bracha took her mother's hand. Mrs. Baker was surprised. She didn't get many gestures of affection from her big daughter.

"Ima?" Bracha almost whispered. "Thank you for a great time. Thank you for the banana split and...thank you for listening." She reached up and gave her mother a soft kiss on the cheek.

Mrs. Baker felt a small lump in her throat. She squeezed Bracha's hand and said, "You're welcome." *And people wonder why I love having such a big family,* she mused to herself.

When they got to the van they saw that the cars on either side of them were gone.

"You won't have to direct me this time," said Mrs. Baker as she unlocked her door.

"I hope not," said Bracha with a broad grin.

Mrs. Baker laughed and reached over to unlock the door on the other side to let her daughter in. As she started the van, Bracha spoke up. "Ima," she said. "Can I ask you one more thing?"

Mrs. Baker rested her hands on the steering wheel and said, "Why not?"

Bracha rubbed her stomach. "Do I have to eat supper?"

Laughing, they pulled out of the parking lot.

"Don't be ridiculous, Donny. She's got to be in the house!" Rivka exclaimed.

"She's not. I looked!" Donny felt panic rising. "I looked and looked!" He tugged at Moishy's arm. Moishy had found *him* — maybe he'd be able to find Saraleh. "Come, Moishy. Let's go and look outside!" Moishy half-rose in his seat.

"Don't go yet, Moishy," Rivka commanded. "Why should she be outside? We'll look in the house first."

"But, but...," Donny tried to protest.

"Everyone can look. Let's fan out." She left the kitchen followed by everyone but Donny.

Donny stared at the kitchen door as it swung closed. She's not in the house. Don't they understand? She could be anywhere! He went over to the back door and peered into the garden, hoping to catch sight of Saraleh.

But I don't think she's in the yard. I looked out all the windows and I didn't see her. Where would she go...?

A picnic! She said she was taking the baby on a picnic! Donny put his hand on the doorknob. Where would she go for a picnic? To the woods?

Donny thought about the woods that joined onto the Bakers' property. He didn't like them all that much. He looked again out of the back door, but he couldn't see the woods from this part of the house. Just then the sun came out from behind a cloud.

Wow, he thought. It stopped raining. Was Saraleh out in the rain?

"This is ridiculous," said Rivka, coming into the kitchen. Donny spun around. Rivka was talking to Zahava. "If she's not in the house, where is she?"

"Where is who?" said Dini.

"Where did you come from?" Zahava asked.

"From the front door. I got a ride home from Mrs. Lederman," Dina told her. "What's going on here? Who are you looking for? I thought after that last game of hide-and-seek you wouldn't want to play for a long time."

"Were not playing hide-and-seek — Saraleh's missing."

Dini's eyes widened in concern. "Are you sure?"

"Yes, we've looked everywhere."

"Even in..." Dini inclined her head towards Donny.

"Even in the blue guest room closet. Moishy looked there." Rivka thought for a moment. "We'd better look outside. I'll call the others." Just then the kitchen door burst open, missing her by an inch.

"Hey," she shouted. "Chezky, will you watch it?"

"Sorry." He came into the kitchen, followed by the others. "We didn't find her."

Rivka told him, "We're going to look outside."

"It's good that it stopped raining," Chezky commented, peeking out the window.

"Oh, my goodness," Rivka exclaimed. "She was out in the rain!"

"Maybe she's in Abba's office," Dini suggested.

"A good idea," Rivka said. "You look there."

Moishy had been staring out the back door. "Maybe she wandered into the woods," he said.

"Moishy, please, don't say things like that!" Rivka's voice was shaking.

"She did; she did!" Donny jumped up and down and shouted. "I know she did!"

"Look what you did," Rivka said accusingly to Moishy. "Now Donny is thinking about such things too!" She turned to Donny. "Don't you worry; Saraleh isn't in the woods. " But she didn't look convinced and neither did Donny.

"She did; she did," he said. "She went on a picnic!"

Rivka ignored him. "Dini, you take care of Abba's office. Zahava and I will do the grounds. Moishy and Chezky split up and go around the block in both directions."

"What about the..."

"When you finish," she said to Moishy slowly and clearly, "then you can check out the trees next to the house."

"You mean the woods?"

"Chezky!" Rivka glanced out the window. "We'd better hurry — the sun's going down.

"Right." The boys and Zahava dashed out the door.

"Rivka, I...," Donny tried again.

"You'll have to stay here, Donny," said Rivka, her voice trying to sound calm and in control. "No one will be able to keep an eye on you."

"Rivka..." Donny looked up at his sister with big eyes.

"Don't feel bad Donny; it's not your fault," Dini added kindly. "You shouldn't have been left to babysit. You're too young." Donny slumped despondently on a chair. Rivka and Dini ran out of the door.

Donny couldn't sit still. He ran to the back door as it slammed. Putting his head against the door, he could hear his sisters calling: "Saraleh! Sa-ra-leh!"

The sun was setting in the clouds. The sky was orange; it looked like it was on fire. I know where she is, and they don't believe me, Donny thought sadly. They said I'm too little. Maybe they think I'm a scaredy-cat. I could find her. It will be dark soon and, she'll be scared. I don't want to be a scaredy-cat... I could find her. Donny stood with his hand on the doorknob.

Mrs. Baker drove up to the house in the deepening twilight. She pulled into the driveway and turned off the ignition.

"Home, sweet home."

"Home, sweet home," Bracha echoed. She sighed happily; it had been the perfect day out.

"Now we'll see what your brothers and sisters have been up to," Mrs. Baker said as she locked the van door.

"It can't be anything too bad," said Bracha. "We haven't been gone that long."

"After that game of hide-and-seek..." Mrs. Baker glanced at her watch. "It's later than I thought it would be. I didn't expect all that traffic."

"Maybe it was because of the rain," Bracha suggested.

"Maybe." Mrs. Baker opened the back door and called, "Hello?"

"Hello, hello!" Yochie bounced into view.

"Hello!" said Tikva from right behind her. "We're glad somebody's home!"

"Where is everyone?" Mrs. Baker asked. She put her handbag down on the *milchig* counter.

"We don't know," Yochie admitted. "We just got home."

"Where were you?"

"Doing *chesed*," said Yochie. "It was an emergency."

"I thought you were supposed to be babysitting," said Mrs. Baker in a low voice. The girls looked uncomfortable. "What's this?" she said, picking up a piece of paper from the counter. "It's a note from Rivka. Now maybe we'll find out where everyone is."

"Here we are!" Mr. Baker walked in the door with Rachel Ahuva in his arms. The baby was holding a stuffed giraffe. "I'm sorry we're a little late, but old Mr. Wein insisted on giving our baby a present. That old softie — when he heard she'd had a birthday, he couldn't resist. We really had a great meeting; we fixed up that deal!"

"I'm glad," said Mrs. Baker. "And I'm glad Rachel Ahuva was a help."

"Should I give her a snack, or will dinner be soon?" Mr. Baker asked. "I think she's hungry." Rachel Ahuva bit her giraffe's head.

Mrs. Baker laughed. "I don't know when dinner will be; I'm trying to figure out where most of the family is." She waved the note at him and started to read it. The expression on her face changed abruptly.

"Is everything alright?" Mr. Baker asked.

"Ima, what is it?" Yochie asked. "You're making me worried."

"Rivka writes that Saraleh is missing. It seems that only Donny was watching her, and she disappeared."

Yochie and Tikva turned pale. "Give me the note," Mr. Baker asked. He read it quickly. "They're out looking for her, " he said. He looked up. "It says here that Donny will be able to tell us the whole story. Where is Donny?"

Donny stood at the edge of the woods, his heart in his mouth. The light was fading; the path could barely be seen. He looked up at the darkening sky and back at the path. A bird flew over his head, and he ducked.

Only a bird, he told himself. He looked at the woods in front of him, dark and dripping. Saraleh is in there, he thought. She's all alone. Maybe she's wet. I'm the only one who knows where she is. I have to go and get her... I'm not a scaredy-cat.

12
Donny to the Rescue

The twilight infused the woods with an eerie glow, silhouetting the trees. The path was damp and in some places slippery with mud; the trees glistened and dripped from the recent rain.

Donny walked on a little-used path. The others had gone to the usual place, but Donny knew that Saraleh hadn't gone there. She was going on a picnic, and he knew she wanted someplace new. He watched the bobbing flashlight beams until they disappeared in the woods. Clutching his own flashlight in his sweaty hands, he continued on his way.

She wouldn't have gone if I'd been watching her, he thought sadly. I went upstairs and she went away. It's all my fault. Now she's here in the woods. And I've got to find her.

There was a scrabbling in the brush, and a small, dark animal leapt onto a tree. From somewhere above him an owl hooted, "Hoooo, hoo-hoo!"

Donny's heart beat faster, and he walked quickly. In a cracked and trembling voice he called out, "Saraleh? Saraleh!" Then he listened; he could hear nothing but the rustling of the leaves.

"Saraleh!" The sky above darkened; the shapes of the trees became vague. What if I get lost? Donny thought. Then we'll both be lost. No, I can find my way. I'm six already. Saraleh's not even four yet. Look, there's a funny stump, and here the path turns. I know where I'm going. I can find my way home.

I'm not a scaredy-cat.

"Saraleh," he called. He could call louder now; his voice didn't crack. "Saraleh!"

He stepped on something soft and soggy. "Yuck!" he cried and jumped away. "What was that?" He looked at the thing from a safe distance. It didn't look like anything.... Wait. He ran and picked it up. It was Saraleh's doll! Tucking it under his arm, he began to run.

"SARALEH! It's me — Donny. I came to find you!" He thought he heard something and stopped in his tracks. Someone was crying!

He ran a little farther, the path curved suddenly, and then, there was Saraleh!

"I found you!"

His little sister saw him and cried even louder. Donny came closer and saw her face was smudged with dirt and streaked with tears.

"Saraleh, I found you. Don't cry anymore." He held up the doll. "Look, I even found your doll."

Saraleh stopped crying and looked up. She took the doll from Donny and tried to smooth its bedraggled hair. "I went on a picnic," she sniffed. "With the baby. It started to rain and I wanted to run home, but I didn't know which way!" She started to whimper again. "I lost my dolly!"

"Don't cry, Saraleh. I found your dolly. I found you!" Donny took her arm and pulled her. "Let's say that I'm the Abba, and I came and brought you home."

"Okay," Saraleh sniffed. She held her doll close and went with Donny.

After they'd walked awhile, Saraleh said: "Donny, can you get home?"

"I know the way," he said confidently. "And Saraleh, I'm not scared. Don't be scared, Saraleh, because I'm not scared, and I'm with you."

"Okay," said Saraleh.

"Here we are!" said Donny as they emerged from the woods onto the Bakers' property. It was almost totally dark. A flashlight flashed in their faces.

"IT'S DONNY AND SARALEH!" someone shrieked. It was Rivka. She yelled to someone else who looked like Chezky. "Tell Ima not to call the police; we found them!" Chezky streaked to the house shouting: "We found them! We found them!"

Rivka ran and picked up Saraleh. She was crying. "Oh, we were so worried! Oh, Donny, *baruch Hashem* you found her! We were so worried about you two!"

"Donny brought me home," Saraleh told her.

"I know my sweetie, I know." She hugged Saraleh close and began to hurry towards the house. "Donny is such a big, brave boy! Come, Donny!" Donny trotted after her as she spoke. "Such a big, brave boy!" she said again.

Donny felt as if he was flying.

The back door flew open and Mrs. Baker hurried out. She took Saraleh from Rivka and held her tight. "*Baruch Hashem!* Rivka, where did you find her? And where was Donny?"

"Donny found her. I met them coming out of the woods."

"Donny found her? Donny, you're so smart. And so brave." Mrs. Baker knelt down with Saraleh still in her arms and hugged him. He stood there with his mother and Saraleh and softly said, "I'm not a scaredy-cat."

"No, my *ziskeit*, you're not," Mrs. Baker whispered. She held him a moment longer, then released him. "You're wet, and Saraleh is sopping," she said. "Let's go into the house."

She stood up and turned to Rivka. "You'd better find the others, especially Abba. They must be frantic. I know I was." Rivka turned to go when they saw Abba coming with the rest of the family.

"Did you find them, Shoshana?" he called. "We can't see a thing. We came back to get a flashlight."

"Here they are!" Rivka screeched, jumping up and down and pointing. Mr. Baker hurried across the lawn, while Mrs. Baker started towards him. "*Baruch Hashem!*" he said. "Where were they?"

"It seems Saraleh went into the woods, and Donny went to look for her," Mrs. Baker told him.

"Donny went to look for her?"

Mr. Baker looked down at his small son. "The other kids combed those woods and didn't see any sign of her."

"I guess you have to know where to look," said Mrs. Baker, smiling.

Mr. Baker picked Donny up and gave him a hug. "Donny, you're great! The whole wide world was looking for Saraleh, and you were the only one who could find her." He put Donny on his shoulders and carried him triumphantly into the house.

Inside, Mrs. Baker took Donny and Saraleh by the hand. "I'm going to get these two cleaned up and in pajamas, and then I'll start supper."

"Oh no, you don't," Mr. Baker stopped her. "You've had enough for one day. Sit down and put your feet up. Zahava, make your mother a cup of tea. Bracha, take Saraleh upstairs, bathe her and put her in pajamas. Rivka, do the same for Donny. Moishy, call Ben-Levi's and order pizza, one with extra cheese, one with mushrooms and whatever you want for the rest. Order drinks too. Tikva, feed Rachel Ahuva some of that junior mush she eats; she can't wait for pizza." The children started to go to their appointed tasks. "Wait!" Mr. Baker called them back. "When the pizza comes, we're having a Baker family meeting. Everyone must be present except those in yeshiva. Now the rest of you clear out of the kitchen; I want to sit quietly with your mother." They left.

Mr. Baker leaned back in his chair and closed his eyes. He didn't say anything until Zahava gave them both cups of tea and left. Then he opened his eyes and said to the ceiling, "Another fun day at the Bakers."

"All's well that ends well," said Mrs. Baker as she sipped her tea.

"I guess so, but I'm not sure I can take much more."

"You've done alright until now." She smiled at him. He sat up and smiled back.

"You're right," he said cheerfully. "And Hashem gives strength." They talked for awhile, enjoying the quiet. Mrs. Baker told her husband about her outing with Bracha. She briefly described Bracha's problem and the plan they'd revised to solve it. He was as gratified as she had been to know their oldest daughter was back on track again.

The doorbell rang. "Is that the pizza?" Mr. Baker asked. "Moishy must have told them it was an emergency!"

Soon the family was settled around the table, Donny and Saraleh squeaky clean and in pajamas. Once everyone was served, Mr. Baker tapped on the table. "All present and accounted for?" he asked.

"Yes, sir!" said Moishy, and saluted. The children laughed.

"Good." Mr. Baker cleared his throat and looked around the room. The mood became sober. "This afternoon, before I left the house with Rachel Ahuva, everyone could be accounted for in the following ways: Ima, at Ho-Ho's. Bracha, at Ho-Ho's. Rivka, tutoring. Dini, packing food. Zahava, helping someone's mother. Yochie and Tikva, babysitting for Donny and Saraleh." At this point, he looked at Yochie and Tikva, who felt very uncomfortable. "Moishy and Chezky, conquering the world, and Donny and Saraleh, playing house." He turned to Yochie. "Now, can you tell me, please, what happened after I left?"

Yochie turned red as she spoke. "Mrs. Freulich called and asked me to babysit. She said it was an emergency, and I figured it was a *chesed*, so I went."

Mr. Baker turned to Tikva. "Then what happened?"

"Yochie was going to do her *chesed*, so I thought I should go to the institute and do mine," she said softly, toying with the cardboard from her pizza. "We told Moishy and Chezky to be in charge."

"I suggested that she go," Yochie confessed.

"Tikva has free choice," said Mr. Baker. "Moishy?"

"Chezky and I finished our Risk game; no one won."

"Stick to relevant information, Moishy."

Moishy cleared his throat nervously. "So we thought that maybe we ought to be doing our *cheseds* too, so we, um, left Donny in charge of Saraleh." Moishy looked down at the tablecloth. "We figured it was only for a short time. Someone was supposed to be home any minute." He ended in a whisper.

"Do you have anything to add?" Mr. Baker asked Chezky. Chezky shook his head.

"Donny, do you want to tell us what happened next?"

Donny looked up at his father. "Can I sit on you?" he asked.

Mr. Baker's expression softened. He held out his arms, and Donny climbed onto his lap.

"I was watching Saraleh, and then I went to my room," he said. "Then I went to get a snack. Some of the kids came home, and I went to look for Saraleh and I couldn't find her anywhere. I looked all over the house. When I was sure she wasn't in the house, I told Moishy, but he didn't believe me." Moishy looked like he wanted to crawl under the table. "No one believed me. They looked all over the house, and they couldn't find her. Then they went to look in the garden. I knew she went into the woods, because she told me that she was taking her dolly on a picnic, but no one would listen to me."

The children all looked sober and ashamed. Donny continued, "They went out to look in all of the wrong places. Rivka told me to wait, but it was getting dark and I was worried!" Here Donny looked at Rivka. Rivka gave him a kind look, so he went on. "I went to that little path in the woods; I thought she went there. It was dark and wet, but I'm not a scaredy-cat." He snuggled closer to his father, who put an arm around him. "I found Saraleh's doll, and then I found Saraleh, and then I came home."

Mr. Baker hugged him. "You're Abba's brave boy — do you know that?" Donny nodded and put his head on his father's chest.

"Abba?" he whispered.

"Yes, Donny?"

"Abba, I'm sorry I left Saraleh. I wasn't a very good babysitter." Mr. Baker looked at his wife. Yochie put her head on the table. The rest of the children looked bleak.

"Donny, *ziskeit*, you were the best babysitter," said Mrs. Baker "You offered to watched Saraleh as your own *chesed* project and you did, even when everyone else left you alone in the house." Donny looked at his mother doubtfully.

"Donny," said Mr. Baker. "A babysitter doesn't have to be with the person he's watching every single second. When I watch you, for example, sometimes I'm in the study and you're in the basement."

"But Saraleh went away!" Donny protested.

"Saraleh knows better than that; it wasn't your fault." Mr. Baker told him. He turned to Saraleh. "Saraleh, are you allowed to go out of the house without telling anyone?"

"No," Saraleh said in a soft voice.

"Are you going to do it again?"

"No."

"What do you say to Donny?"

"I'm sorry, Donny."

"Okay, Saraleh," Donny sat up and squirmed.

"Not only were you a good babysitter, Donny," Mrs. Baker continued. "But you were responsible even afterwards."

Donny stopped squirming.

"You were worried about Saraleh and you went to find her, even though it was scary in those dark woods."

"I wasn't scared," said Donny softly and comfortably.

"I guess not," said Mrs. Baker. "You found her, and we are very proud of you."

Donny smiled from ear to ear.

"Just one thing, Donny," said Mr. Baker. "Rivka left us a note, and that was a good thing to do because then we knew where everyone else was. Next time, leave us some kind of message. We were worried about you too!"

"Okay, Abba."

Mr. Baker squeezed Donny, then turned to the rest of the family. "Well, my friends, here we have it. Everyone runs off to do *chesed* leaving the six-year-old to save the day. Can anyone tell me what went wrong here?"

There was an awkward silence. Then Yochie spoke up. "It's like you were saying before, I mean the other day, you know, last week, I think..." Mr. Baker nodded for her to go on. "Whenever it was. We have to get our priorities straight. We have to learn what is more important and what to do first."

"Good. Any other ideas?"

"I thought that *chesed* was *chesed*. That it's a mitzvah and it comes first," said Tikva. "I never realized that you sometimes have to choose between *cheseds*."

"Me neither," said Rivka. "I think we need some rules on how to choose."

"The Torah gave us some rules," said Mr. Baker.

"Do you mean like: '*Bnei ircha kodmim?*'" Moishy asked. "The people of your own city come first?"

Mr. Baker nodded.

"I guess that in this case it would be: '*Bnei beischa kodmim*'" said Zahava thoughtfully. "Those of your own household come first."

"That's right," Mrs. Baker approved.

"What else?" Mr. Baker asked.

Bracha spoke up. "You have to make sure that what you're doing is really a *chesed*." Mr. Baker nodded at her to go on. "You could be doing something that you think is helping someone, when actually you're doing more harm than good. I learned about this recently. Someone was asking to copy my homework all the time. I thought I was helping her because she isn't a very good student. I thought maybe she could learn from my homework. But in the end she was only using me and not trying for herself, so what I was doing wasn't really a *chesed*."

"I never thought of that," said Dini. The rest of the family nodded in agreement.

"My *chesed* didn't work out very well either," said Moishy with much chagrin. "I think I bothered Great-Aunt Frieda more than I helped her."

"And then she slaughtered you in chess," Rivka chortled.

"You played chess with Great-Aunt Frieda?" Mrs. Baker asked him. "Didn't you know that she's the Bloomfield Jewish Community Center's senior citizen woman chess champion? She slaughters everyone!"

"Now they tell me." Moishy groaned and put his head in his hands.

"Do you really think that you bothered Great-Aunt Frieda more than you helped her?" Chezky asked him.

"Yes," Moishy answered from between his fingers. Chezky looked thoughtful.

"Sometimes *chesed* can be really hidden," said Yochie, thoughtfully. "When I first went to my babysitting job, I wondered why the lady needed me. She has a big, beautiful house, and she's very organized." Yochie rolled her eyes to the ceiling. "But she needed help alright."

"*Chesed* doesn't just fall in your lap," said Zahava. "I had to look hard to get my *chesed*."

"Sometimes you get more than you give," said Dini softly.

"*Chesed* is an *avodah*," said Rivka. "It sounds so easy: You just go out there and do it, but really you have to think a lot and do hard things. And you have to be very patient," she added with a smile.

"I think we're learning," said Mr. Baker.

"Abba did a *chesed* today," said Mrs. Baker.

"Yeah, it was great that Abba took care of Rachel Ahuva!" said Yochie enthusiastically.

"It was great that Abba did that, but that wasn't what I was thinking of," Mrs. Baker told them.

"What were you thinking of?" Dini asked.

"Mr. Wein, Abba's client, can sometimes seem a little brusque, but he's really a nice man. He's lonely. He adores Rachel Ahuva and was thrilled to see her."

"But he did a *chesed* for her!" Rivka protested. "He bought her a giraffe.'

"Maybe she did a *chesed* for him by accepting that giraffe?"

The children thought about this. "I think I see what you mean...," said Dini.

"Anything else?" Mr. Baker asked.

"We've said a lot!" said Yochie.

"We certainly have," said Mr. Baker. "And learned a lot too. But there's one more thing that has to be said."

"Oh, Abba, we're sorry!" Yochie ran to the head of the table and hugged her father. The other children apologized too.

"Well, that's that," said Mr. Baker.

"Not quite," said Mrs. Baker. Everyone turned to look at her. "I've decided that, for the time being, I'm postponing our outings." Everyone's faces fell. "At least until the end of the great *chesed* project," she amended. "However, tomorrow everyone is grounded. No one is allowed to leave the house, no matter what!" She eyed the children. "Because I am going on one more date."

"With who?" asked Yochie.

"Donny," Mrs. Baker announced. "I think our hero of the day deserves a trip to Ho-Ho's."

Everyone heartily agreed.

That night as Chezky got ready for bed he watched his little brother thoughtfully. Donny lay on his bed. He had a small car with him and was driving it up and down his pillow, humming softly. Even though he was supposed to be asleep, Chezky decided not to make an issue of it; it had been a big day.

He looks so small there, thought Chezky. Just like he looked that night after he'd been locked in the closet. Boy, was he scared. I wonder if anyone realizes just how much it took for him to go into those woods. He's been through a lot.

After he was in his pajamas, he went down the hall to brush his teeth. Coming back, he paused with his hand over the light switch. "Should I turn off the light, Donny?" he asked.

"Why not?" Donny asked. "I want to go to sleep." He put his car under his pillow and turned over to face the wall.

"Me too!" said Chezky. He smiled at his little brother's back and flicked the switch.

YOU'RE INVITED

To a quintuple celebration!

Rivka, Zahava, Dini, Tikva, and Yochie Baker
would love to see you at their upcoming
Bas Mitzvah extravaganza

When: Sunday, June 18th, the 9th of Tammuz,
at 3:00 P.M.
Where: The Baker lawn
On the Menu: Fun and surprises galore

So put on your party hats --
and see you there!

Something terrifying is coming to
Bloomfield...
he Baker's Dozen will never be the same.

s when Moishy, Chezky, and Yochie Baker open a small detective
r the neighborhood kids. Little do they know that they'll soon have a
ystery to solve — one that involves the sinister plans of a group of
ted terrorists. The trail of clues will bring the Baker boys perilously
close to the edge of disaster!

OPERATION
FIRESTORM

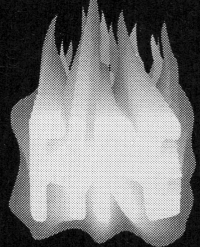

A three-part Bloomfield mini-series.
Look for it at your local bookstore.
It's a story you'll never forget.

A TARGUM PRESS BOOK
Distributed by Feldheim Publishers